WHAT PEOPLE ARE SAYING ABOUT STRAIGHT OUTTA EAST OAKLAND2

I have rarely seen a man **say so much** *to our lost generation of urban youth with so few words! Our young people gravitate to Harry because he dresses like the streets he talks like the streets but more importantly he* **listens with pure love**, *complete lack of judgement, and total presence as our students confide in him about doubts and dreams they are too afraid to share with anyone else. I have seen countless souls in baggy jeans and black hoodies* **weighed down by a violent past** *ask to go to Harry's office only to come back to my classroom empowered with self-confidence and determined to be agents in their own positive transformation. The daily preaching that Harry does with ears and heart ensures that the preaching done with his mouth remains* **real and genuine** *for the hip hop generation.*

ANTOINE LEGARDE
San Francisco high school teacher

Reverend Harry Williams **speaks the truth** *with fervor and authority. His commitment to making a difference in the lives of inner city teens permeates who he is and what he stands for. As his intern at the Glide Memorial Church, in the notorious San Francisco Tenderloin, I was blessed to observe the reverend at work,* **radically touching the lives** *of people with real-life problems. Acting out his faith and values, his life is a vessel for peace on the urban battlefield. The commitment demonstrated by the reverend* **touches all who hear him** *on the streets, in the prisons and in the pews. He altered the course of my life by encouraging me to become a teacher in an urban school system. I am truly thankful for his* **straight-talk ministry** *and brotherhood in Christ.*

CHARLES LEE
San Francisco high school teache

D1411454

With what seems to be all the intensity a great writer can possibly muster up, Harry Louis Williams II has done it again. In his writing he **masterfully creates the boldness of the streets** and the realness of the people who occupy them. His writing is so powerful and sharp, so convincing and moving. The way he **brings the reader into the world** he so passionately writes about is fascinating. Harry Louis Williams II is not only a great writer, he is a great thinker.

SARAH O'NEAL RUSH
Founder and Executive Director of the
Booker T. Washington Empowerment Network

Harry knows and loves Oakland. **His heart beats for reconciliation**, peace, and justice. You can see it in his friendships, in his work, and in his writings. Harry is a great friend to us who care about the city. He's a bridge builder – **connecting people with wisdom** and generosity of spirit.

JOSH McPAUL
Pastor, Oakland City Church

Harry Louis Williams II is a prolific urban fiction writer who has **captured the essence of street life** and culture in his book Straight Outta East Oakland II: Trapped On The Track. This book is a riveting page-turner that captivates and skillfully guides the reacher into the dark crevice of the inner city. The main character, Firstborn Walker, finds himself in the midst of a violent dilemma, **trapped between two worlds**, one filled with gang violence, drug dealing, and the unglamorous life of innocent young girls being pimped out as sex workers in the human trafficking market, and the one world that would fulfill his desire to live a **peaceful and productive life**. Williams is a masterful artist whose name will one day be spoken in the same breath as Donald Goines and Iceberg Slim. Straight Outta East Oakland II: Trapped On the Track is a must and recommended for teachers, outreach workers, social workers, and more importantly, clergy persons who endeavor to minister effectively in the inner city.

REVEREND PAMELA M. WILSON
Minister of Evangelism, Allen Temple Baptist Church, East Oakland

Straight Outta East Oakland: Trapped On The Track *is a story that gives off the* **powerful aroma of truism** *for the life of a young black woman...I mean GIRL who's vision of life is handcuffed to the lives of the Devil...profoundly working through what she might think is her savior, a pimp named Phenomenal...because her existence dictates pain, tragedy, and hopelessness. As a survivor of the bright lights of lies and promises of a man whose motives kill your soul...*Straight Outta East Oakland *gripped me as* **I felt the rush of my blood** *and heat of from the rapid beating of my heart as the memory of my journey to salvation and FREEDOM was captured on the pages of this book...the* **consolation of a true Savior**...*Jesus Christ...soothed my soul! Professor Williams, as I call him, is a true professor of the urban grip of hopelessness on the lives of our people who struggle for existence in a world that is so demanding of "survival" by any means necessary. Professor Harry Williams, like Paul, has been called to people separated from God due to their minds being blinded by the god of this world...Thank you, Professor for* **proving hope** *by speaking in the language of those of us who have been trapped in the grip of deception. This book is truly phenomenal!*

JEANETTE COOKS
Marriage, Family Therapist (MFT)/Trainee,
Certified Addiction Specialist (CSA)

We need to listen to Harry Williams. He combines the wisdom of a veteran minister and social worker with the cultural competency of a hip hop aficionado. He is a revolutionary leader and a **powerful preacher** *and author, yet he is humble and gracious. As many other young Christian leaders, I look to Reverend Harry for guidance and encouragement. He is* **not afraid to speak the truth**, *whether it is to young people in our ghettos or to older people sitting in church pews. May we hear his message and* **be inspired to follow Jesus** *into the gritty streets of East Oakland and similar neighborhoods! We need to hear the message that God has given him.*

NATE MILLHEIM
Founder and Executive Director of Shalom of Oakland

STRAIGHT OUTTA 2
EAST OAKLAND
TRAPPED on the TRACK

a novel

HARRY LOUIS WILLIAMS II

SOUL SHAKER PUBLISHING
OAKLAND, CA
WWW.SOULSHAKERPUBLISHING.COM

Published by:
Soul Shaker Publishing
Oakland, California
www.revharrywilliams.com

© Copyright 2011, Harry Louis Williams II
All rights reserved

Printed in the United States of America
First Edition

ISBN: 978-0-9789133-1-1

Cover and interior design © TLC Graphics, *www.TLCGraphics.com*
Cover by Tamara Dever, interior by Erin Stark

DEDICATION

This book is dedicated to several groups of people:

- The young folks from the Bay Area's hardest hoods who attended the Glide Memorial Church/YouthBuild Program in San Francisco.

- The teachers and support staff who gave so much of themselves.

- My neighbors here in East Oakland. Thank you for keeping me safe and making me feel loved. You are the best.

- Rest in peace Teena Marie aka "Vanilla Child." Your music has made the world a sweeter place and we are grateful.

- The Miracle Factory Network, true believers who have made my dreams come true. There are still good people left in this world. You can find them at *www.TLCGraphics.com*.

- Finally, this book is dedicated to any person trapped in an abusive situation, especially sisters trapped on the track. Never let anybody make you believe that you are not somebody and that you do not matter, because you do. God loves you.

** In Oakland, the terms "blood" and "cuz" are rarely used to denote gang affiliation.

"JUST WHEN I
THOUGHT I WAS OUT,
THEY PULL ME BACK IN."

CHAPTER
ONE

SOMETIMES A KNOCK AT THE DOOR CAN CHANGE YOUR LIFE. I was cramming for my biology exam when that knock came for me. Assuming it was one of my knucklehead dorm mates who had forgotten his front door key, I jogged to the apartment door in my bare feet and swung the door open without question.

Since it was fairly dark in my room, the hall lights blinded me for a moment. When my retinas had adjusted to the light, the hollow eyes of a living ghost glared back at me. The ghost cleared her throat and then clicked her dentures. She rocked back and forth without saying a word or making another sound. A verse from the Bible flashed inside my cranium: "Be sure your sins will find you out."

"Would you like to…? Do you want to…?" Funny, I could hardly make the words come out. She clasped her hands behind her back and stepped forward. The scent of old, wilted orchids wafted past my nose as she strode past me. She had dropped a good 50 pounds since the last time I'd seen her. The coloring had gone out of her hair, leaving it pearl white. There was no embrace, no handshake. Once inside the apartment, she turned toward me. For what seemed like a solid minute, she just stood there in a faded maroon jogging suit that bore the words, "God Is Good – All The Time," across the front. She stared right through me.

"Would you like to have a seat, Ms. Holmes?" I asked. I gave a sweeping gesture that ended at a folding chair in front of our meal table.

"No thanks. I'll stand. What I got to say won't take long."

I could hear the low hum of banter and laughter in the hallways. Young men and women coming in from the college commons and the local pubs joked and flirted. I tried to recognize some of the voices – anything to take my mind off the horror that had tracked me down.

I had tried to put the past behind me. Still, sometimes screams pierced through my nightmares. I would wake up shivering, my sheets damp and my hands shaking. But the memories had begun to fade. The past is gone, I would tell myself.

Apparently, it was not. For here, right in front of me, stood someone I had once deeply wounded.

Ms. Holmes gripped the back of the folding chair, leaning on it for support. Her frail body shook. Finally, she gave up. Ms. Holmes yanked the chair out from under the table and gingerly sat down on it. She glared at me with a toothy smile and whispered in her best graveyard voice, "You killed my baby, Firstborn."

"I know," I responded. "That is, I didn't mean to kill her. I really didn't kill her." My thoughts and words jumbled together. My hands rested flat on the tabletop. And then the trembling started. It began at the base of the wrists, and then it spread to all 10 fingertips. Ms. Holmes smiled. She reached across the table and placed her cotton-soft hands on top of mine. Her palms were cold and clammy. Her own eyes narrowed, and though her lips twisted into a slight smile, her eyes never did. Her words hung in the air like mace.

"You killed my baby," she said again.

"I didn't kill her," I whimpered. "At least I didn't mean to...."

"YOU KILLED MY BABY!" she hollered. "I trusted you. I believed in you, and you led my daughter away from home, crack dealer. You turned my little girl out and put her on whore stroll, and when you got done with her, you left her to rot, dead in the street like an old stray cat done been hit by a car!"

Then she let out a high-pitched shriek that could have made your eardrums bleed. I plugged my ears with my fingertips until she ran out of breath.

Ms. Holmes abruptly lifted her hands and banged the tabletop with her fists. Tears crested in her eye sockets before making tiny waterfalls on her cheeks.

I was frozen in my chair. There was another knock at the door. I jumped up and ran to see who was there. I opened the front door slightly. Dina, the mousey dorm attendant, stood staring back at me with an upraised eyebrow.

"Is everything all right in there, Firstborn?" she asked, as she craned her neck to look over my shoulder. I did my best to block her view.

"Yes. Everything is fine, Dina. Ahh, ahh, Auntie came up from Oakland to tell me that my old next-door neighbor passed on. Everything's fine," I lied. "Go on back. Go on back, now."

Dina didn't budge. I don't think she believed me. I had to practically shut the door in her face. If Ms. Holmes didn't keep her voice down, I could see myself getting thrown out of San Jose State U. I walked back to the dining room table. Ms. Holmes was leaning over the table, hunkered into a ball.

"I didn't kill her, Ms. Holmes, but God knows that if I could go back into the past and make a different decision than the one that I did, I would. I didn't kill Maggie. I didn't put her out on the track. Another low-life did that. He's dead now. But not a day goes by that I don't think about Maggie with sorrow and regret. I wish there was some way I could make this right. God knows, I wish there was something I could do."

Ms. Holmes' shoulders heaved as she sobbed. With some effort she straightened her back. She slipped a bony hand inside of her huge, black plastic purse and extracted a photograph not much bigger than the size of postage stamp. She reached out for my hand and then gently pressed the photo into my sweaty, trembling palm. I looked closely. Staring back at me was a cocoa-complexioned young girl with bangs and a broad smile that lit up her face. She was wearing a gray-and-white plaid Catholic school uniform.

"In fact, there is something that you can do. That's why I'm here," Ms. Holmes continued.

"Who's this?" I asked.

"That be Lisa, my grandchild. You remember her. They call her 'Crayon.'"

In fact, I did remember her. Crayon was a cute little girl who always wore bib overalls. Her mother and father were deep in the game. Whenever their daughter got in the way of their plans to get money, they ditched her at Ms. Holmes' place. It's ugly, but a lot of people do it.

I felt sorry for Crayon. She always looked so lonely. Crayon never seemed to have any friends. No one ever came by the house to visit her when she was living with Ms. Holmes. When I'd come to visit Magdelene she'd be sitting at the kitchen table with a crayon in her hand drawing portraits of famous people. She was quite good at it as I remembered. Once she drew a picture of the civil rights activist, Ella Baker. It looked just like her. I told Crayon she should pursue art as a career. She smiled when I said that. I wasn't just talking. She was a brilliant kid. I remember looking at her report card. It had straight A's.

Crayon was 14 years old the last time I saw her. She used to call me "Uncle Firstborn." Anything can happen, yet she was the last person I could ever imagine selling her body in the streets. I caught a lump in my throat.

Ms. Holmes continued as if on cue. "The child's father ended up in Soledad on a strong-arm-robbery charge. Her mama was fighting a "harboring a fugitive" case. I wasn't mentally stable enough to take care of the child, not after what y'all did to my baby, Magdalene."

Ms. Holmes coughed and snarled before she continued. "CPS took her. She ended up in foster care. From there she landed in a group home. Something happened to that child. It was like the childhood vanished from her eyes one day and she was a grown woman. I asked her what was wrong, but she wouldn't talk about it. I called the CPS worker. She said she would look into it, but that was the end of it. The next thing I knew the woman was knocking at my door talking about, 'Lisa done run away from the group home. Is she here?' Me and that child used to be close, Firstborn. We were more than grandmother and grandchild; we were friends, and she didn't call for a month. I was worried sick. I was thinking all kinds of things. And then Mother Rainey came into church one day with tears in her eyes. She asked me to leave the Sunday school class and meet her in the ladies' room. She say, 'I think I just drove past Crayon. She on ho stroll.'"

"What did you do then?"

I hollered out, "Jesus, Jesus help me." And then I got in my car and high-tailed it out to the street where the prostitutes walk day and night.

"Did you see her?"

"I waited a half an hour. I waited an hour. And then I saw my baby. Her head was drooped down. Her hair was done up nice. She had on a too-short dress and some high-heel pumps. I hollered out, 'Lisa baby, get in this car. Grandmama wanna take you home.'"

"And then what happened?" I asked.

Ms. Holmes' spine curved into the chair like it had just turned into jelly. She aimed her face at the ceiling light. She stopped blinking. Only her lips moved.

"Firstborn, she didn't even flinch. She just looked down at the sidewalk like she was a zombie or something. Lisa was always an obedient child. It wasn't like her to ignore me. But then I saw *him*."

"Saw who?"

"That sleazy, bottom-feeding pimp, that's who. Reddish-colored boy with long blond dreads tied back in a rubber band. They call him Phenonmenal. I ran over to Lisa and grabbed her hand. It just went limp, like there wasn't no muscles in it. That's when he, he...."

Ms. Holmes winced as she recounted this part of the story. I couldn't breathe. "That's when he what, Ms. Holmes?" I asked.

Her eyes had yet to blink. She continued, "He pushed me away. He said, 'Crayon, you wanna go with this old lady or you wanna be with your man?' Crayon looked down at her shoe tops. She didn't say nuthin'. I tried to grab her again. That's when he did it."

"Did what?" I asked.

Ms. Holmes sat up to stare right into my eyes.

"That's when he slapped me in the head with his gun."

"Oh, sh...," I sputtered.

She nodded and smiled. "Yes, now you see the picture. I fell down on the ground. I had on my Sunday go-to-meeting dress and my brand new black church hat. He hurt me, Firstborn. My head was bleeding. How could he do that to an old lady?"

I shrugged my shoulders, speechless. I could picture the scene. Her nightmare had become mine.

"Firstborn, when I tried to get up again he waved his finger at me like he was saying, 'Don't do it, old lady.'"

But I wasn't going to let him steal that child if I could help it. I made it to one knee when he kicked me down with his boot. Then he yanked Crayon's arm and hollered for her to get in the car.

"'He ain't your daddy, Baby. You ain't got to listen to him!' That's what I hollered, Firstborn. But you know what that son of a bitch said? …'xcuse my French. He said, 'Her blood daddy in jail. Now I'm her daddy.'"

I didn't know what to say, so I just nodded and she went on with the story.

"She looked so lost, Firstborn! I called CPS. I called the cops. They had her arrested – not him but her. They took her from juvenile hall back to the group home. She wasn't there a week before she ended up on whore stroll again. It's like a merry-go-round. Now, the papers say there's a serial rapist what's out preying on these young girls and cutting them up. We got to get a hold of my baby before that fiend gets to her."

We?

Ms. Holmes buried her face in her hands. Tears leaked through her fingers. "I didn't raise Crayon like that, Firstborn. She a good girl. I think that pimp, Phenomenal, got her drugged up or hypnotized. That nigger is inside her mind."

Ms. Holmes' eyes took on a pleading tone. She licked her lips, struggling to make the next words come out.

"Firstborn, I want you to bring my baby back home."

My jaw dropped open. Instinctively, I moved back from her.

"And don't look at me with those puppy dog eyes," she continued. "These people up here at this college don't know who you are. I used to think you were a nice boy, too, but you're a gangster. You can make people do things."

My heart did a triple pump. "Ms. Holmes, I'm not in the streets anymore. That part of my life is over. I get good grades here. I'm planning on becoming a journalist. I even go to church sometimes."

She cut me off. "The Bible say, 'Can a leopard change its spots?'"

"People change, Ms. Holmes. People change," I said.

"But you ain' changed, Firstborn. People talk about that band of thugs you used to run with. I believe you call yourselves the 'Black Christmas Mob?'"

This lady is out of her damned mind, I thought. I started meditating on the quickest way to get her out of my apartment and on her way back to Oakland.

"I can't do it, Ms. Holmes," I said.

"Come back to East Oakland and save my grandchild," Ms. Holmes went on.

I took a deep breath. It was my turn to grab Ms. Holmes' hands. Clasping them between both of my own, I said, "Ms. Holmes, I know you're a serious church lady. You wouldn't want me to come back to Oakland and do something wrong, would you?"

Ms. Holmes leaned forward and whispered, "Son, in the hood sometimes we have to do a little wrong in order to get some right out of life. Sure I want you to come back. You can bring my baby home."

There was another knock at the door. I assumed it was Dina, again. I had no choice but to ignore it.

"Don't you wonder how I found you, Firstborn?" Ms. Holmes asked. She had tucked her combat voice away. She was speaking in natural tones now.

"It wasn't easy finding you. Folks said you just vanished off the face of the Earth. But the Lord works in mysterious ways, his wonders to perform. One of the children from back in Oakland goes to school up here. She told me she saw you in the cafeteria one day. You don't know her but she knows you...or at least she knows who you are. Just as easily as I found you there are others who could find you up here, some who would pay money to find out where you are."

Ms. Holmes hoisted an eyebrow so I wouldn't mistake her intent. Finally, she stood up from the table. She pointed her finger in my face. I resisted the urge to slap it away.

"I figure you owe us for what you did to my baby. I'll be looking to hear from you, Firstborn."

Ms. Holmes pulled her car keys out of her purse. She nodded, and then she showed me her back and walked out. A line from one of the Godfather films flashed through my mind: "Just when I thought I was out, they pull me back in."

"AFFILIATES AND ENEMIES ALIKE ENDED UP DEAD. INNOCENT BYSTANDERS CAUGHT STRAY BULLETS. AND I WAS RESPONSIBLE...."

CHAPTER
TWO

WHO COULD I TALK TO ABOUT WHAT HAD JUST HAPPENED? NO one, not my roommates, not the girl I was seeing at the time, not one of my new college friends…no one.

That night I lay back in bed with my fingers laced behind my head. Sleep was a stranger. I blinked hard as the montage of my past exploded on my mind's screen. I saw myself sitting in front of a triple-beam scale with a folded ace of spades in my hand. A loaded Glock 17 lay in my lap with the safety clicked off. Ice Cube thundered in the background, "Bow down to the game lord!"

Next, I saw myself on the corner in front of the liquor store directing the movements of my crew as they served the fiends. We were hungry and the money was fast. It was do or die and a lethal glue of greed and loyalty bound me to the niggas I had come up with. As they say in the streets back home in the Town, "Yeah, we was gettin' it."

As I lay there that night, I saw the boss of the Black Christmas Mob, Drama – my best friend since childhood.

Drama's relatives on his father's side were Native American. That's where he got the long hair that he often wore in a ponytail. He became the closest thing that I had to family after my grandmother died.

Drama's childhood dissolved after his father, a preacher, was gunned down by the police. He had been an A student. But after he was expelled from high school, Drama became the type of thug that your favorite rapper is portraying in those videos.

Drama never backed down from anything. He was known for two things: the loyalty he showed to his friends and his gun game.

How did I get trapped out there on the turf? I had been the one who had stayed in school and made all the right choices. However, when the day came that I needed money to stay alive, Drama was there. When the chance to go to Allston University presented itself, Drama gave me a chance to make the money I'd need to supplement a scholarship. I had been a square all my life. But I got down with him and our homeboy Street Life. I was broke, damn near homeless. I really didn't see a choice at the time. (Looking back, there's always a choice.)

As I twisted on my bed in the dorm that night, gunfire blasts exploded in my memory. I saw visions of dead homies staring back at me from R.I.P. T-shirts. Fear gurgled in the base of my stomach like a virus. It all went bad. I had barely escaped with my life. Yet, through the grace of God, I wound up at San Jose State University. I was a few years older than most of the students in the dormitories, but a college diploma doesn't list your age. I was in it to win it.

I was finishing up my junior year, holding a solid A average. I played on the badminton team. I kept my mouth shut and my nose in the books. I didn't even listen to gangsta rap anymore. I developed a penchant for Beethoven. I had recently begun dating a young lady that I liked a lot. Her name was Caitlin Bennington. She walked up to me one day while I was studying in the library and just said bluntly, "I'm feeling you, dude."

I had never even seen her before, but as I got to know her, it seemed that we had everything in common. I kept conversation centered on the present and the future. I became an expert at dodging questions about the past. I didn't ask about hers, and she didn't ask about mine. Things were going lovely.

If you've been following my story, then you know why East Oakland would be the last place on Earth I'd ever want to go back to. What Ms. Holmes had said was true: Endonesia, one of our enemies, already had a murder-on-sight order out with my name on it.

Latin Caesar, the don of the Guns, Cash, and Dope clique, had warned me to stay out of East Oakland. He promised me a coffin overcoat if I ever got down with the brothers I grew up with. Latin Caesar was the last dude in Northern California that you would want to be beefing with. He and his goons would definitely squeeze a trigger on you.

Add to everything I just said the fact that last time I saw my old clique they were pointing guns at my dome, and you'll realize why I wasn't anxious to help out Ms. Holmes.

I hadn't been to Oakland in close to a year and had no plans on ever going there. Oliver, my mentor, was the only person in Iraq, Hellafornia, that I remained in touch with. The last time we spoke he told me he'd met up with Drama at a red light and he'd asked about me. Oliver didn't tell him a thing.

I was kind of surprised that Drama had been able to survive a green light order from the GCD set. There was money on his head, too.

There had been a time when I would have jumped in front of a bullet for Drama, but that day was done. He had betrayed me. As for me asking him to help with this situation? It wasn't going to happen.

It would have been easy enough to ignore Ms. Holmes. What could she have done? Drag me back to East Oakland? Still, there are some things you can't run from. When you're in the streets smoking weed, getting with the females, ripping and running, you don't sit still long enough to come face to face with yourself.

When you step out of the streets and your world slows down, you start remembering things – things you're sorry for. I felt guilt about what happened to Magdalene. If I hadn't brought her into the game, she would probably still be alive and well today. She was dead too young. And I had loved her.

Maggy wasn't the only one. Lots of others had lost and paid the price. I had used a triple-beam scale and Pyrex pots to make it snow in the hood. People I grew up with like family ended up strung. Little girls and boys became orphans. Affiliates and enemies alike ended up dead. Innocent bystanders caught stray bullets. And I was responsible – at least in part. What if there was a chance to make at least some of that right? Shouldn't I go home and cleanse my conscience?

As I lay in bed that night, I made two promises to myself. First, no matter what happened I would not be the cause of physical harm striking anyone. Second, I was coming back from East Oakland alive after I safely returned Crayon to her grandmother. Still, I couldn't sleep. The faces of murdered black people kept flashing before my eyes.

CHAPTER
THREE

THE NEXT DAY I HOPPED THE 4:04 P.M. AMTRAK TRAIN FROM San Jose to Jack London Square in Oakland. Everything looked so different in the high-rent district. New condominiums had sprung up where once warehouses stood. The sweet aroma of Everett and Jones barbecue reminded me that I was hungry.

I didn't have money for a plate of ribs and collards. I had transformed from block sav to college student, and with that reinvention comes some budgetary constraints. There was no money for a sit-down meal, but I did have enough in my pocket for a fat burrito in the hood. I took the bus downtown, and then I hopped the International Boulevard bus heading for the heart of East Oakland.

The bus zoomed past the Serenity Funeral Home, Gorilla Zeke's Tattoo Parlor, Big A's Tire Store and Rim Shop, Freedom Now Bail Bonds, Pay Day Loan Check Cashing, Get Paid Quick Pawn Shop, the Get High Smoke Shop, and the Glamour Girls Nail Salon. It finally stopped in front of my favorite taco truck, the one that said "Mexico City" on the side with the painted palm trees on it. I used to eat there every day. I hadn't sampled one of their extra meat steak burritos in almost a year. I jogged up to the counter. Drool came to the corners of my lips as I made my order.

I was counting out quarters when I heard car tires squeal in the middle of the street. A driver in a black Mazda was busting a U-turn. "It's a hit!" I said out loud to no one and dove behind a nearby parked car. As I hit the pavement someone hollered, "Firstborn!" The voice was friendly.

My heart beat like a jackhammer. I picked myself up off the concrete and brushed the dirt off my knees. My hands trembled a little.

War Thug, a Black Christmas Mob affiliate pulled up to the curb next to me. He leapt out of the car and ran toward me, arms wide. His long dreads were tied behind his head with a giant rubber band. He wore a carefully trimmed goatee. His Oakland Raiders jersey looked brand new. His black jeans had a razor sharp crease.

They called him War Thug because he lived for beef. If you were in the streets getting it, but you weren't about what you said you were about, War Thug might want see you about that. I once saw him make a gangsta strip in the middle of a house party. He robbed him because the fool had double-parked alongside his car, making it impossible for War Thug to pull out into traffic. And as Thug was fond of saying, "Time is money." War Thug had some rough edges, but he was good people. He was loyal to a fault. We had been friends since kindergarten.

War Thug threw his arms around me. The sun reflected from his gold teeth when he opened his mouth. "What up, godfather? I ain' seen you in like forever!" he said.

He read my clothing unconsciously. I was wearing a knitted sweater with a white button-down shirt underneath. I sported gray slacks and black dress shoes.

"Damn, homie, why you dressed like Tiger Woods out this piece?" he said, scoping me from collar to shoes.

"It's a little hard to explain," I said. Anxious to change the subject, I asked, "How are our dudes doing?"

"The game is the game, and the game don't stop, man. Black Christmas Mob be bangin' and slangin', reppin' that hood all day, word to God," he said. "It's crazy, man. We got the most active hood in Oakland. We spreading like the plague. BCM is everywhere…. You seen the big homie, Drama, yet?"

The man behind the counter handed me a paper bag with a burrito in it. I hadn't counted on running into any of the Mob members, which is silly when you think about it. I was coming home, and they certainly hadn't gone anywhere.

I had mixed feelings about looking up Drama again, though. Nine months ago he'd left me to die in a pit of killers. When War Thug mentioned his name I just shook my head.

"Drama done grown to be a major factor in these streets, my nigga," War Thug said. "Nigga ridin' around in a brand new silver Infinity with a Bose sound system. He got diamonds on his fingers, and he got them fingers in everything. Don't nothin' move in our hood that Drama ain't got a hand on it. Drama rollin' with bodyguards and the whole nine, nigga. We got dope spots all over the East. Niggas tell Drama a whole lot, but they never tell him no."

War Thug pulled out a business card from his pants pocket. He handed it to me. It said, "Situations Handled." There was a phone number on the bottom.

"Is this Drama's phone number, War Thug?" I asked.

"Drama don't use no phones…. I know something major went down between the two of y'all, but he still your brother. I never seen anybody get as close to him as you. When you get ready to see the big homie, call this number. Somebody on the other end of this line will hook it up. Get at your potna. He gon' be glad to see you, watch."

"Does Drama still hang out at the same places?"

"You won't see him just walkin' around like before," War Thug said. Drama's hot, baby boy. The Mob got enemies everywhere."

"So, who's runnin' the hood, now?"

"I said 'you don't see Drama walking around the hood.' I didn't say he wasn't runnin' it...."

War Thug's eyes scoped up and down the block.

What you drivin', Firstborn?"

"I took the bus down here," I said.

"The bus? The AC Transit bus? Nigga, I ain' rode the bus since 10th grade. Oh, man, you better call that number. A dude like you, useta gettin' it like we get it, ain't got no business ridin' the bus! You better call that number right now. He reached in his pocket and extracted his phone. He said, "Here, use my cell."

"Naw, man. I do need a ride though," I said pointing at his Mazda.

"You ain't said nuthin' but a thing. Let's go."

We walked over to the car. War Thug popped the locks and we hopped inside. I started munching on my burrito.

"Where we headed?" he asked as he put the key in the ignition.

I gave him an address on MacArthur Boulevard. War Thug reached beneath his shirt, and a black .9mm pistol came out from hiding. He slapped in a fresh clip, clicked the safety off, and then loaded a round in the chamber. He put the gun beneath his seat before we drove off.

"What's that for?"

"You been gone an eternity in these streets, godfather. We got enemies over there now."

"It's like that though, Thug?" I asked, pointing at the spot where he'd slipped the nine.

"This is the O, godfather. Out here niggas don't respect nothin' but hot lead and dead presidents." The Mazda roared away from the curb. Sideshow Psycho's new joint, "Body Bag 'Em," thundered from the trunk.

> *I load up the clip and let off a round*
> *Leavin' that fake nigga underground*
> *I had to blow him out his socks*
> *Now he food for the worms inside a box*
> *Black Christmas Mob rolling thick and deep*
> *Hood respected, makin' mamas weep*
> *Stacking paper to us is quite vital*
> *Just ask the hood god Dramacidal....*
> *Fools talk a lot but I don't respect 'em*
> *Got my sneaker buried deep in dey rectum....*

"I COULD HEAR SOBBING
IN FRONT OF ME.
CRAYON WAS STILL TRAPPED
IN THE SLAVERY OF PROSTITUTION."

CHAPTER
FOUR

Dark clouds had fallen on East Oakland as we pulled up to Ms. Holmes' building. Young brothers milled around the corner inspecting the insides of passing cars. The Mazda pulled to the curb a few feet away from the bunch. I took a deep breath and grabbed my backpack. The thugs in front of the building stiffened.

"I'm coming inside with you, godfather," War Thug said. He wasn't asking. He opened his door and stepped out on the sidewalk. I could feel the short hairs rising up on the back of my neck.

He checked his gun one more time. The pistol slipped back in War Thug's belt band and then got shielded by his shirt flap. Slowly we walked up to the three-story apartment building. Four young black men with dreadlocks blocked the door. The tallest wore a black baseball cap turned backward. "What y'all want around here?" he asked.

War Thug spit on the ground. "Bro, we ain' got no problem with you. We just goin' to visit somebody."

"Who?"

War Thug's eyes blazed with anger. "None of yo' damn business. Who is you? The police?"

"Look at that tat on his neck, y'all," the tall kid said.

War Thug had a BCM tattoo on the side of his throat. I heard a low whistle as the four examined it. I could sense others joining the group in front of the building. This was new. The year before, I walked in and out the building to visit Maggie without a problem. Now, this spot was Ground Zero in a war zone. The block had grown hot and dangerous. War Thug put his hand on his .9mm. He spoke to me without turning around.

"You see. That's why I don't come around here, godfather. You see how niggas act?"

The tall one looked us up and down and started cursing us. "You ain't the only one strappin', potna."

He wasn't lying. Two of his friends pulled up their shirts. I saw the handle of a Mac-11 and the butt of a .38 revolver. Damn. I should have stayed in San Jose, I thought.

War Thug pushed me behind him. We were now encircled by an arc of death, but ghetto instinct told him to put himself between me and potential danger. This scene wasn't new to him. Shootouts are a consequence of the game. It was said that in the hood, you better leave the house wearing clean socks because you never know. You might tie your shoes in the morning, but the coroner might be untying them at night.

At that moment, the front door of the building opened. Ms. Holmes' bedroom slippers flip-flopped as she trotted toward us.

"It's all right, young Willie," she said waving off the tall one. "These boys are friends of ours."

Willie must have been the tall one. His eyes squinted. He measured Ms. Holmes with a look that could have passed for compassion and then nodded. The crew took the cue and slowly drifted back toward the corner. In places like Oakland, your friends and affiliations can get you killed. My cold, clammy hands trembled as I thought just how close I had come to meeting my Maker. I hid them in my pockets.

Ms. Holmes was grinning and crying at the same time. Her voice cracked when she spoke. "I prayed to God that you would come, Firstborn. And you're here – our angel of deliverance." She squeezed my face between her warm, sweaty palms, and then she kissed my forehead.

War Thug scratched his scalp in bewilderment but said nothing. Ms. Holmes leaned forward and whispered, "I got a call from Mother Reyes. I told you she lives out there where Crayon be at. She say she's out there now, Firstborn. You go get her. I'm going to go upstairs to make the bed for that child."

She turned away and started back up the stairs, still talking out loud, this time to herself. "I'm going to make that child some French fries and a hamburger. That's her favorite meal. I got that Pebbley Poo body wash that she like…."

We watched Ms. Holmes raise her hands above her head and shake them in praise to the Lord. "Glory!" she shouted. "Glory!"

War Thug and I walked quickly back to the car and hopped in. He put the Mazda in gear and zoomed away.

"Where to now, godfather?"

"You ever heard of a pimp they call Phenomenal?"

War Thug was silent for a few moments. His lips pursed together in a tight line. "Why you back here, godfather? Talk to your nigga, now. What's up?" he asked.

"I need to talk to this pimp named Phenomenal. You know who he is?"

War Thug shook his head from left to right and back. War Thug sucked his teeth. "Phenomenal," he said. "Real name,

Ernest Allen. Child soldier, abandoned by his strung-out 13-year-old mama and raised by the streets. Nigga used to sleep in abandoned buildings and under stairwells. He ate what other people threw out. One day, a d-boy offered some real paper if Ernest would bust a slug in this other nigga' ball cap. What a hungry nigga won't do for food! From that day on, he was a ghetto terminator, puttin' in work for the hood.

Now he's grown...probably 22 years old. He went from sleeping in a ditch to being hood rich. They call that nigga, "Phee." Pimpin' is just his sideline. That nigga Phenomenal is straight psychotic, and he got hittas on the block holding him down. I'm talkin' 'bout some live Town niggas. They pushin' a real line out here. They 'bout smash-and-grab jewelry store robberies, house licks, home invasion, gun sales, dope sellin', pimpin', hits for hire, you name it. He got a older brother they call Black Hole, either because he always be at the Raider games in the black hole seats or because if you mess him, he'll put you in a black hole. That nigga is a giant, and he ain't playin'."

"I just want to talk to Phenomenal."

"Talk to him! Godfather you can't talk to no nigga like that. We gotta get the soldiers. We gotta get deep and then roll up on those niggas like mercenaries. All they understand is gun smoke. Phenomenal don't have no fondness for strangers walkin' up on him wanting to hold conversations. Killers like Phee will blow a nigga's brains out, then ask questions later."

"Well, I have to try," I said.

"You ain' even got a banger on you, do you?" War Thug countered.

I shook my head no.

"So, you just want me and you to..."

I cut him off. "Not me and you – just me. I want you to take me out where he is and just keep rolling."

"Well, that's just what I'm not going to do. If I let something happen to you, where would I live? Drama would hunt me down and kill me. So, give me a plan B."

"Wait for me, but don't get out of the car no matter what happens."

"What?"

"Man, I don't want any more violence. I'm done with that. I'm about non-violence now. I don't want anyone else to get hurt because of me. So if something breaks out, just drive away. Swear to me."

A blue Mustang cut us off at the corner of 51st and International. War Thug sped up, trying to catch the driver. He cursed the man like he had lost his mind.

"Thug, swear to me," I said again.

He put his fingers together and said, "Boy Scout's honor."

I was dead serious and here he was playing around.

"War Thug, will you stop?" I hollered. "You were never a Boy Scout!"

He grinned out loud.

It was hardly dark, but the track was alive with enslaved humanity. Young girls, black, white, Latino, Native American, short, tall, plus size, and thin; girls ages 14 to 25 walked slowly up and down the bustling street. I tugged Crayon's photo from my shirt pocket and cupped it in my hand. I showed the image to War Thug. We drove up and down for about 20 minutes, and then I felt the car slow down. My heart jumped as we came to a stop.

War Thug tilted his head down and pointed. "Look," he said.

And then I saw her. She bore little resemblance to the girl in the photo. Some twisted soul had dressed her up in a cheerleading outfit and high heels. A white man in a black SUV slowed down and said words to her that I couldn't hear. She winked at him. They began to bargain.

"That's her, Thug. Get up close and let me out. And remember, whatever happens, don't get out of this car."

"What?"

"Nigga, I said whatever happens, don't get out of this damn car!"

"Be careful, homie," War Thug whispered. "Phenomenal ain't going to be too far behind his money tree. Be quick and don't sleep."

I jumped out of the Mazda and ran up to Crayon before she could get into the SUV. I kicked the trick's car door shut. "Do it wiggling, creep. Get up out of here." The old man put his car in gear and sped off.

Crayon stared at me in disbelief. "What you do that for? That's money you just chased away."

"Crayon?" I asked, not hiding my shock.

Her tone changed three pitches when she responded. "My name, Lollipop," she said popping gum. "I don't know nobody named Crayon."

I opened my palm and showed her the picture.

"Don't try to play me, girl. You know who I am. Your grandmother sent me, Crayon. She's afraid for you. Come on, sweetheart. We have to get out of here, now."

Crayon's brow wrinkled. Worry throbbed in her voice. "Uncle Firstborn, you have to get out of here. Go and don't look back. Hurry up!"

"I'm not going anywhere without you," I declared.

Crayon's eyes opened wider. A blob of chewing gum fell out of her mouth.

He was on us before I could move. Rage turned his face red. He spoke to her like I wasn't even there.

"Bitch, didn't I tell you never to look another nigga in his face!" he shouted. His blonde dreads flew up in the air when he threw a bolo punch to Crayon's stomach. She doubled over. Her right knee hit the ground. Her eyes flickered in terror.

There were two of them: the man with the blond dreads and gold Rolex and a heavy muscled juvenile in a wife-beater with a dragon tattooed on his neck.

By talking to Crayon without a pass, I was playing with their money, and I too would have to be dealt with. That's the streets. Phenomenal drew closer to me. His eyes were searching my pockets and waistline for the imprint of a pistol. I think he was surprised that I was out there unarmed.

"Homie, you ain' come down here to face down some real niggas without a hammer in your hand, did you? Why you out here runnin' your mouthpiece at my ho?" he asked.

I ignored his questions. I was outraged.

"Fool, you hit her like she was a man. She's a little girl. She's only 15 years old!"

"So what, Captain Save A Ho?" he asked through gritted teeth. "What's that to you?"

"I'm her uncle. No human being should be treated like this," I said.

Phenomenal laughed. "Don't feel sorry for these bitches, my nigga. These weak-minded hos need a manager. They are incapable of running their own lives. That's where I come in. I am a scientist of pimpdom. Once I fall off into a chick's domepiece it's all over. If I tell her to walk away from her mama and her kids and never look back, she'll do it. I got a bitch like your niece here locked in a state of pimpnosis. If I threw doggy biscuits in a bowl and said, 'Eat it,' she'd get down on her knees, eat the dog food, lick the bowl, and then look up and say, 'Thank you.'"

He was impressed with himself. He threw his arm across Crayon's shoulders and kept preaching. "You see unc, she all about his pimpin' and I'm all about this paper. The two go together like biscuits and gravy."

I stretched out my hand and grabbed for Crayon's finger-tips. "This is my niece. Her grandmother wants her home."

Looking back at it, he had to have been surprised by my sheer nerve. The brother in the wife-beater started pounding his fist into his palm.

"She ain't goin' nowhere with you, lame. We on this money hype and you throwin' mud in the game," Phenomenal said. He grabbed the crook of her arm and stared at me through his shades.

I took one step toward them.

It was then that the young dude in the wife-beater whirled me around by the shoulder, a major violation in these streets. His eyes looked wild and psychotic. When he smiled, I noticed that his two front teeth were broken. "Ay, yo Phee, I seen this boy somewhere before," he said, scratching his head.

"What turf you from? What street you claimin', nigga?" he demanded. I ignored him.

"Phenomenal, I'm here to take this girl home. She's only 15 years old."

Phenomenal put his head down like a bull and started crowding me. I pushed his shoulders.

The dude with the dragon tattoo on his neck gave me an upper cut to the belt line. I felt like I'd been hit with a can-nonball. I smashed him in the nose with a straight jab. So much for the non-violence stand.

Phenomenal caught me with a right cross. I threw an elbow that landed across both his eyes. At that point, I was searching for a brick or a bottle. That's not fair, you say? In the streets the only rule is kill or be killed. I kneed Phenomenal in his tes-ticles. He bent over and screamed.

I didn't see the punch that knocked me down. I blacked out. When I woke up they were kicking my ribs and stomping my forehead. "Jesus, help me," I prayed.

Phenomenal was out of breath. "Yeah, you gon' need you some Jesus comin' out here conversatin' with one of my hos, taking food out of my mouth...." That's what he said before he stomped his foot down on my chest.

"Hey, Phee, I remember where I seen this cat before!" the young man in the wife-beater said. "He used to be with Drama and Chopper and dem niggas – them Black Christmas Mob fools."

"Chopper?" Phenomenal laughed. He began to say the ugliest imaginable things about our dead homie. I cursed him.

Chopper had been shot to death during a holdup at an after-hours gambling spot. I wasn't there, but they say he jumped in front of a bullet to save Drama's life. Drama never talked about it. However, he did have Chopper's name tattooed on his right arm. And now, Phenomenal was talking about our fallen brother like he was some sort of sucker.

Phenomenal and the boy in the wife-beater were dragging my limp form. The concrete ripped my back. I was too beaten up to moan. They were trying to get me behind a building. Then Crayon screamed.

I heard a car door slam. I couldn't see who it was. My eyes were swollen shut, but they say that the hearing is the last thing to go. I heard somebody holler, "Black Christmas Mob fo' life, niggas!"

It was War Thug. He had broken his word. A .9mm pistol hollered, "Buck! Buck! Buck! Shoe leather slapped across the sidewalk. Phenomenal cussed Chopper one last time.

I heard a car speed off. War Thug grabbed the crook of my arm and hoisted me to my feet. I stumbled, struggling to keep my balance. "I told you to stay out of it," I whispered through bloody, swollen lips.

"Is you retarded, nigga! What you think I got this banger fo', to make a fashion statement? What you thought, I was going sit back and let them off-brand niggas murk you? That'll never happen and that's on everything. Firstborn, you a strange nigga, sometimes."

I climbed back into the shotgun seat.

"Where you wanna go now, man?"

"Take me back to Ms. Holmes' crib."

War Thug sucked his teeth and shook his head as he pulled us a way from the curb. "Godfather, did I hear that fool holler something about our dead homie, Chopper?" he asked.

I held my forehead with both hands. "I think so," I answered.

War Thug hollered, "We need to get Drama. We gotta get the soldiers. These fools put hands on you and they need to be dealt with. And this nigga disrespecting our dead homie?" War Thug shook his head. "Oh, no. We can't let this go like that. Uh-uh. Hell, no."

I shook my head, no. The inside of my mouth was sore. My left eye throbbed with pain. I could still feel size 11 bruises on my ribs and thighs.

"That's not going to happen, brother. Don't even tell Drama that you saw me, let alone about what happened today. Take me back to Ms. Holmes' house," I said.

We drove back to MacArthur Boulevard without a word between us. It was quiet in the car except for the sound of War Thug's teeth grinding together. He wanted to go back there and kill something. How could I explain to him that I had changed? He sure hadn't.

Ms. Holmes was standing in front of the gate of her building when we pulled up. Her pink house slippers flapped across the cement when she raced toward the car. A shadow of sadness and horror fell over her face when she peered into the back seat and found it empty.

"Where is she?" she asked, heartbreak ringing in her voice. I had no response.

War Thug reached over and opened my car door. "Godfather," he said, "when you get tired of getting your ass beat, call that number and niggas will get dealt with; that's on my mama and my kids," he said.

War Thug yanked a blunt from his shirt pocket. He stuck it between his lips and lit it. He blew a cloud of smoke over my head. Then he started the car and cut his eyes in my direction, "I'm out, my nigga."

I turned to find Ms. Holmes staring holes through me. "Did you see my baby out there, Firstborn? What happened?"

I sucked my teeth, exasperated. Didn't she see my black eyes and bloody lips? What did she mean, "What happened?" The streetlight over my head flashed on while I gave Ms. Holmes a rundown on what had happened. I told her everything except the fact that I saw Phenomenal bolo punch Crayon in the stomach like she was a man. That would have devastated her.

"Lord, have mercy," she prayed as I got to the part about the stomping.

"We need to get you to the Highland Hospital emergency room."

"What for? If something was really wrong, I'd be dead before they called my name. I ain' 'bout to be sitting up in some hospital all night so they can sell me a hundred dollar aspirin. Just let me rest for a minute. I'll be all right."

Ms. Holmes opened the gate. We walked through the front door of her building and then into a lobby that was lit up like Times Square on New Year's Eve. I had to squint to protect my eyes from the brightness. Everything hurt as I followed Ms. Holmes up the steps. I could hear her sobbing in front of me. Crayon was still trapped in the slavery of prostitution. I had been beaten up badly. And Drama knew I was back. Could things get any worse, I wondered.

In fact, they could get worse. Much worse.

CHAPTER
FIVE

THE TELEVISION NEWS BLARED IN THE BACKGROUND. "THE Oakland Police Department was called to the scene of yet another homicide – this one in broad daylight at the corner of...."

Ms. Holmes switched the channel. The *Wheel of Fortune* reruns were easier on her nerves. How were we going to get Crayon off the corner? That was the question. I pulled out my cell and punched the number as soon as the thought hit me. I took a deep, peaceful breath as soon as I heard the voice.

"Hello."

"Hey, its me," I said.

"Hey what's up, me? How's college life? Still pullin' down them A's."

"College life is fine. It's this other problem that I have."

The voice sounded suddenly bone weary. "Firstborn, this problem you got, does it have anything to do with biology or journalism?" the voice asked.

"No."

"Does it have anything to do with San Jose State University?"

"No."

"Oh, no. Boy, you sound close."

"I am close."

"How close."

"East Oakland, close."

"Damn," Oliver muttered. That was the first time I had ever heard him curse. "Where you at?"

I gave him an address.

"I'll be there in 10 minutes. Don't move."

No problem there. I couldn't have moved if I had wanted to. Everything hurt.

Oliver was like my big brother. He called every week to pray for me. He helped with my school supplies. He was more family to me than any of my blood relatives. I had met him one day when I was running from the OPD Task Force. If there was one person on the planet who was on my team, it was Oliver. I could tell that I had let him down. What else could I have done? I was the co-creator of the monster called the Black Christmas Mob. A lot of people were dead because of that, including my ex-girl Magdalene. If I could save Crayon's life, shouldn't I have tried?

Twenty minutes from the time we hung up the phone, Oliver was knocking hard at the door. Ms. Holmes went to let him in. I could hear the conversation.

"Hello, my name is Oliver. May I speak with Firstborn, please?"

His dreadlocks had grown a little bit longer, but other than that, it was the same Oliver. His wife, Liza, was behind him. I liked her. A foot shorter than Oliver, Liza was Oliver's gentler half. She taught third grade. Shock registered on her face when she saw my wounds.

"Boy, what happened to you?" she exclaimed.

Ms. Holmes told them the whole story.

"You mean you couldn't come to me?" Oliver asked. "Son, you have all the book learning in the world. God bless you for that. But you ain't got no hood sense at all. That ain' the way you handle a problem like that."

"How do you know?" I asked.

Oliver answered my question with a question. "What does that tattoo on the side of my neck say?" It read: DEEP EAST OAKLAND.

Do you know this pimp?" Oliver asked.

"No."

"So you just gon run up on a total stranger in a hot zone, talking 'bout 'I'm taking your young money-making ho away from you.' And here you are dressed like a prep school dropout. It's only the grace of God that fool didn't blast you!"

"What should I do?" I asked. "And sit down. Y'all are scarin' the hell out of me. It looks worse than it is."

"What do you want to say to this girl, Firstborn?" Liza asked.

"I don't know…. Let's try, 'Come home. Your grandmother wants to talk to you.'"

Ms. Holmes had been standing by listening, still as a statue. Liza squeezed Ms. Holmes' hand between hers. "Mother, may we have a pad and a pen?"

Ms. Holmes reached in a drawer and grabbed a notebook and Bic pen. She handed them to Liza who handed them to me.

"Sit up, Firstborn. You're a writer. Write something that would introduce yourself. Something intriguing. Invite her to reach out to you."

I was puzzled. "Liza, why should I do this?" I asked. "How can we even get a message to her?"

Liza said, "Leave all of that to me. You just write."

In East Oakland, where nothing is quite what it seems, I stopped asking questions. I thought for a minute, and then the words came rolling out.

"Hello, Crayon:

"This is your uncle, Firstborn. Let me get straight to the point.

"Crayon, I think that you are a woman of worth and endless possibilities. I believe in your future. What could I possibly know about what you are going through right now? Last year, I was deep in the streets. Today I'm a college student. My goal is to one day write books. Who knows? Maybe one day I'll write a book about you.

"I'd love to talk to you. I want to talk to you about your goals and your dreams. Your Aunt Maggie would have wanted us to be friends. I just want to talk to you, not preach a sermon. I believe in you. I want to help. Call me."

I scribbled my phone number at the bottom of the paper, and then I handed the note back to Liza.

Liza folded the note in half and stuck it in her purse. "I'll make sure she gets it," she said.

"How?"

"Firstborn, I love ya, but you're not only square, you're a nosy square. Relax, baby. I got it handled."

Oliver stood up.

"Come on, Firstborn. Let's gather for prayer."

I knew that was coming. Oliver was a true believer – a hardcore thug turned hardcore Christian. He was as real about his faith as he had once been about his gun game. I respected him more than any preacher I had ever met, except maybe Drama's father. I wasn't all the way in yet, but I was listening and studying. I was paying attention. I was almost ready to make a commitment to the Lord. Almost.

"You want to lead us in prayer, Firstborn?"

"No, Oliver. You've been doing well in this department so far."

"Son, you better learn how to pray for yourself. Oliver ain't going be here always."

I shook his hand with my eyes closed.

"Yes, you will. Don't say that. Now go ahead and pray, OG." He fought back a smile.

"Father God, they say back in slavery when black folks was traded like cattle, the master would uproot a person and set him down in a new slave community full of strangers. Those folks would take that stranger and turn him into family. Well, Lord, Firstborn is our family. I love him like a brother. Like a son, Lord. There's something special about Firstborn, Lord. I sense an anointing on his life. God, he ain't always as serious about his life as he should be. Because these fools out here don't know the value of life, and they'd just as soon shoot you as spit on the sidewalk. Lord, bring him through this situation. Lord, I'm asking you to touch this young girl..."

"Crayon's her name," I whispered.

"...Crayon. God, remember your black people and your brown people, your Cambodians, your Samoans, your poor white people, indigenous people, people without legal status or documentation, women and children hiding in the shadows, ducking from the INS. Lord, bless EVERYBODY suffering in the hoods and trailer parks of North America. In Jesus's name. Amen."

We were quiet for a moment. Oliver grabbed me about the shoulders and hugged me. He patted my back. It hurt. Liza squeezed my ribs and kissed my cheek. That hurt, too.

"We have the annual church picnic tomorrow. Wanna go?"

"Sure, why not?"

"We'll pick you up about noon. And remember, son, we're here for you. If you need us for anything, just call."

I smiled, but I was sad inside because I had failed. Tonight, Crayon would be in the streets forced to perform sexual acts on strangers. Would she get beat up or cut up? Would she catch some disease, I wondered. And had my coming to Oakland merely served to make her situation worse? I limped back to the bedroom and then fell on the bed and into a black chasm of sleep.

CHAPTER
SIX

I AWOKE TO THE SIZZLE OF FRYING BACON AND SCRAMBLED EGGS.
My eyes struggled to acclimate themselves to the darkness. I
had that feeling of disorientation one faces when waking up
in a strange place. Voices whispered and warbled from somewhere beyond the closed bedroom doors. A knock startled
me, and then the door cracked open. Ms. Holmes spoke into
the darkness. Even though I couldn't see her voice, I knew
she was smiling.

"She's here, Firstborn, she and her friend. Get up and come
on out."

There was no need to ask who had arrived. Apparently,
somehow Liza had been true to her word. I jumped out of bed
and reached for my khakis, which lay neatly folded over a chair.
My stomach flipped as I pulled my shirt down. What would I say
to her? Without a clue, I strolled into the living room barefoot.

There she sat at the kitchen table in the same clothes she
had been wearing when I spotted her out on the track the day
before. Her hair was combed and teased. Her nails were

sculptured and painted. The scent of cheap perfume barely covered a long night of sexual activity. Bags had begun to form under her eyes.

Crayon's high heels stuck out beneath the table at an angle. She took a swig from a Coke bottle, and then she reached deep into her purse. She extracted a black hourglass. She flipped it upside down so that all of the sand was on the top. For a moment we sat motionless, watching the grains trickle down to the bottom.

"When the sand all reach the bottom, me and Sapphire got to be back where we live," she said.

I didn't have to ask who had given the order. I did ask, "So, where do you stay?"

She ignored me and took another swig from the Coke bottle.

The young woman sitting at the table beside Crayon was about the same age but not quite as pretty. Her hair extensions were beginning to unravel. Her eyeballs shook with fatigue and terror. Though she looked 30, she was probably 17. When our eyes met, she started chewing on her fingernails like a mouse gnawing on yesterday's newspaper.

Crayon reached out for one of my hands. She had yet to look me in the face. She twisted my fingers around and began to rub them between her hands.

"Your hand is swollen and all bruised up. You got two black eyes." She hadn't mentioned the lump that rose up from my scalp like Mount Everest.

"You must be very brave or crazy. Phee might have killed you yesterday," Crayon said.

I could hear the sounds of pots and pans jostling in the kitchen. The fragrance of fresh brewed coffee made my stomach growl. Ms. Holmes was singing, "Leaning on the Everlasting Arms."

"I got your note last night. It was nice. Nobody talks to me like that...anymore." Crayon's face spread into a sad smile.

I could hear the eggs and bacon crackling in the frying pan, and the smoke was beginning to drift out of the kitchen. I had never realized that a bad beating could make a man so hungry. I licked my lips in anticipation. I could hear the bread being slammed down in the toaster. The refrigerator opened. I imagined that Ms. Holmes was retrieving the orange juice and the strawberry jelly.

The poor child next to Crayon licked her lips, too. I wondered when she'd last had a good meal.

"What's your name, sister?" I asked.

"Sapphire," she said.

"Nice to meet you. My name is Firstborn."

She smiled. "Firstborn, that's a funny name. What does it mean?"

I broke it down. "My mother died giving birth to me. They say that the last thing she said was, "first born." So, they gave me that as a name. My father used to say that I represented a new day for black people. He'd say, "Boy, you are the firstborn of a new generation.""

Ms. Holmes walked out of the kitchen gingerly balancing three heavy plates. Grits slid off the edge of my plate. I reached for the salt. I can't eat grits without salt, butter, and pepper.

"Uh-uh. Put down that salt, Firstborn. Did you know salt kills more black men than bullets? You ain't even taste the food and you puttin' them tiny poison pellets on it."

I grabbed my fork and plunged it into the eggs.

"And I just know you aren't going to put that food into your mouth without saying grace."

I already had a mouthful. I was embarrassed.

"I wouldn't think of it," I mumbled.

Crayon and Sapphire both giggled.

"Say the grace, child," Ms. Holmes said nodding briefly at Crayon.

"God is great, God is good, and we thank Him for our food. Amen," Crayon recited.

Half of the sand in the hourglass had already spilled to the bottom.

"Crayon, I saw a picture that you'd drawn in the room down there. It was of Angela Davis.

She blushed a deep red. "Oh, that. I was just messing around." I slurped down some orange juice. "No, it's good. It's really, really good."

Her eyes brightened. For the first time they met mine. "Do you really think so?" she asked.

"Mmm-huh," I said while breaking my bacon into pieces. "Girl, you got skills. Why don't you pursue art, Crayon? You have a gift."

"Can't think about that now, Uncle Firstborn. I wish I could. That part of my life is over."

"What about you, Sapphire?" I asked. "What do you want to do with your future?"

She munched on a sandwich she'd made with the bacon and eggs. "I used to dream about going back to high school. Now, I just think about making it from one day to the next. It ain't safe for us to have many dreams. They might find out and…."

I knew it was none of my business; however, the words had leapt out of my mouth before I could stop them. "Sapphire," I asked, "how did you wind up in the game?"

She rolled her eyes at the ceiling as if she was contemplating whether to answer or not. And then she just shrugged. "My stepfather was a damn crack head. He was always trying to put his hands on me. One day he told me to take the newspaper over to Wardell's place. Wardell was a low-life piece of street trash who used to lay up with Effie and her kids in the apartment across from ours. He used to drink and smoke up her check and then beat her when it was all gone.

"When I knocked on the door, Wardell told me, 'Come inside.' Three of his friends was there. Wardell say, 'Your stepdaddy owe me $200. You here to pay his bill.'

"I tried to run but they grabbed me and forced me into the bedroom. I was a virgin, and they.... "

I cut her off. I didn't want to force her into the pain of reliving that experience. "What did your mother do?" I asked.

"Who you think used to smoke crack with those devils?" she said. "Mama told me, 'Barbara,' that's my real name, 'you're a woman now. It's best to put some things behind you.'"

"How did you end up in Oakland?" I asked.

"MySpace," she said. "A man said they were looking for models. I always wanted to be a model, Uncle Firstborn. He wrote me and told me to meet him at the Greyhound station in Oakland. The modeling agent turned out to be Phenomenal. Now, I do all my modeling on the track for tricks. I came up here when I was 15. I'm 16 now."

Crayon smirked, "So? There are chicks out on the track 10 and 11 years old."

"Why don't you just run away, Sapphire?"

Sapphire shrugged her thin shoulders. "Where would I go? Besides, I'm scared. I don't want to end up like Betty."

"Who's Betty?" I asked.

Sapphire dropped her fork. Her eyes grew wide. She shifted her gaze toward Crayon and began to stutter. "Betty, Betty, uh...."

Just then the last few grains fell to the bottom of the hourglass. Crayon and Sapphire jumped to their feet. Crayon raced over to squeeze her grandmother's neck. Sapphire bowed and said, "Thank you." And then they raced out. The front door shut with a bang. I shivered involuntarily.

Ms. Holmes was crying again, her shoulders drooping. We both stood there motionless, staring at the door like we were waiting for the two girls to return through it.

Finally, Ms. Holmes broke the silence. "How's the food?" she asked.

I had lost my appetite, but I said, "Fine."

Crayon had left her half-empty Coke bottle on the table. I stuck my finger into the top of the bottle and rubbed some of the liquid on my tongue. It tasted bitter and sweet at the same time. I spit the sample out into a napkin. "Bo," I said. "I knew there was something in there!" The Coke was spiked with Promethazine and codeine cough syrup. They call it "Bo" in the Town.

I walked the bottle over to the sink and poured it out. I said nothing to her grandmother, who eyed me curiously. I guessed that Crayon had started "leaning" (that's what they call it) to take away some of the mental pain of streetwalking.

Ms. Holmes lifted her fists toward the heavens and shook them. "Oh, God! First Maggie and then my Crayon. Lord, how much more can I take?"

I walked over and put my hands on her shoulders. Her head flipped toward me as though I had just brought her out of a trance. For a moment, just for a moment, I could have sworn I saw a trace of deep-seated hatred in her face. Then, as quickly as it had appeared, it vanished.

CHAPTER
SEVEN

IT RAINED THE NEXT DAY. NOW, IF YOU LIVE IN CLEVELAND OR Harlem, you might not think that strange. However, if you live in California, you'll appreciate the irony. You see, in California we have a rainy season that ends in April. It hardly ever rains in the summer, hardly ever. This was an omen.

At 12:00 p.m. on the dot, Oliver stood banging at Ms. Holmes' front door. He was stomping his wet sneakers on the doormat when I opened up. My friend was cloaked in a yellow rain slicker with a matching hat. Droplets of rain dripped from the tips of his thick mustache. "What type of weather did you bring us, boy?" he asked.

Oliver glimpsed over my shoulders at Ms. Holmes, her slender form slumped over the table. "Hey there, Ms. Holmes!" he hollered.

She fought to forge a smile. The corners of her mouth twitched, and she just gave up. The light evaporated from her eyes. She stretched her arms out across the kitchen table, clasping her hands together. She dropped her head down, lost in her own world of misery. I was fearful that her sanity was leaving her. And of course, I would have to carry some of the blame for that.

Oliver brought me back from the webbed complexity of my own thoughts. "Young blood, we gonna chow down today! You ain' never had my Liza's fried chicken have you?"

I shook my head as I followed Oliver out the front door and down the stairs. A drizzle of unwelcome tears formed in the corners of my eyes. "No, I don't think I've tasted Liza's chicken." The tears started dripping fast now. I didn't feel cold, but I started shivering just the same. My soul was quaking inside of me. I felt so alone. Spiritual exhaustion fell on me like a wave.

Oliver looked back over his shoulders at me. "Be strong, young blood. Be strong." I had wiped my face before we hit the first floor landing. Still, the tears flowed. When I opened the building's front door, a gust of Pacific wind rushed at my face. My tears mixed in with the rain.

Liza sat in the shotgun seat shaking her dreads to Kirk Franklin. She turned to face me when I opened the back door. "Firstborn," she said, alarm ringing in her voice, "what you doing? Crying, sweetheart?" How she could tell my tears from the raindrops was a mystery.

"It's nothing," I said. "Really, nothing."

Liza turned around and faced the mean streets of Oakland. Oliver pulled us away from the curb. "You really shouldn't have come back here, Firstborn. There's nothing at the end of the road you walking but a smoking pistol and an early funeral."

"I had to come back," I said under my breath.

"No, you ain't," Oliver said quietly. I could hear anger mixing in with his disappointment.

"You could have called me and asked me to handle it," he said.

"I'm a man. I made this mess. Now I have to fix it."

Oliver stared at the road ahead, but he was shouting at me in the back seat. "Fix it how? These niggas you going up against got guns. You lucky to still be alive this long."

I was angry at myself for crying. I was so frustrated. I felt responsible for what had happened to Crayon. I also felt helpless to do anything about it.

Liza started humming, something she did to calm her husband whenever he lost his temper.

Oliver snorted. "Whatever the hell you do, don't even think of calling your boy Drama. That would be like trying to put out a forest fire with gasoline. Stay away from those Black Christmas fools, you hear me, Firstborn?"

He was begging more than asking. But Oliver didn't have to worry. I was done with Drama. Nothing on Earth could ever get me back with the boss of the Black Christmas Mob. Nothing.

For a few moments we rode through East Oakland in silence. Down MacArthur Boulevard and then left on 81st Avenue. Past ramshackle shotgun houses, two-story box-style apartment buildings, liquor stores, funeral parlors, and churches. The string of buildings repeated on Bancroft like the background loop on a cartoon. Then right on 98th.

Soon we started to ascend Skyline Boulevard. The houses grew larger and more opulent. The streets got cleaner. We sprinted past wooded groves and tree-lined streets. A deer peeked out from behind a huge oak tree. The sirens ceased their everlasting whine. The screech of the speeding drivers slamming brakes was gone. The police ceased their troubling. Even the rain clouds lifted. We were in the Oakland hills.

If you and I were standing in front of a liquor store on 81st Avenue and International, with dope fiends hunting their next blast and hitters scoping out targets all around us, you probably wouldn't believe that there was a forest with sliding boards and picnic tables two miles uphill. And yet here we were.

The scent of barbecued ribs tickled my nose. It took my mind off things. Oliver and I grabbed two big pans of fried chicken and a tub of potato salad that he and Liza had loaded into the back of the Range Rover. I started salivating.

This was the Greater Grace Church family picnic. I had had a bad experience with these folks. When I visited there the pastor had tried to put Drama and me on blast. He tried to humiliate us. I thought he was too cold-blooded to be a preacher. He presided over Negroes who had made it and thought they were better than the brothers and sisters back in the hood. Sure, they might have rode in Jaguars and Benzes, but did that mean they were better than people like me who rode the AC Transit buses?

I couldn't trip over that now. It was going to be a good day, I thought. And I needed a break.

I was contemplating these things when Oliver shouted, "Firstborn, you know I'ma roast you on the court today, don't you?"

I chuckled, "We'll see, old school. We'll see."

Did he really think he could take me to the hoop? Oliver was in his late 40s, and he was starting to spread out around the rib cage. I was still in my 20s, and I had a crossover dribble that could break his ankles. Thinking about it made me laugh.

"What you laughing at, young blood?" he asked.

"You'll see when we get on the court," I said, giggling at the thought.

About 100 members and friends of the Greater Grace Memorial Church lounged on benches, smoking cigarettes and chewing the fat. A few nodded in our general direction as we set the fried chicken and potato salad on the table.

I licked my lips. Liza's fried chicken had company. I saw a pan of collard greens, several plates of hamburgers and hot dogs, more fried chicken, and of course, watermelon.

A heavy-set woman with a white sun visor and a T-shirt that said, "Lincoln Family Reunion-Broward County," sat guard over the table. Her ham-sized forearms folded over her ample gut.

I mustered up the courage to ask, "May I take a piece of chicken, Miss?"

She scowled, "We ain't said the grace yet…."

"Does that mean, no?" I asked.

She looked at me like I was the biggest idiot ever to take a breath on God's planet Earth.

"You can wait," she said with a snort.

Liza moved up behind me. I turned to see an angry smile stretched across her face. She squinted at me as she spit out her words. "Boy, I paid for that chicken. If you hungry, you can have a piece."

The woman scowled, "But it ain't been prayed over!"

Liza reached forward and pulled up a corner of the tinfoil cover. A fat chicken leg speckled with black pepper sat on top. "I prayed for it when I was frying it," she said.

I was glad to have that little teaser because it would be another hour before the preacher showed up, and nobody was going to eat anything before he pronounced the grace over the food. I thought, is he the only one that can say a prayer? What did they do at home, play a recording of his prayers before eating? It was silly to me. That's why I had a hard time buying into the whole faith in God thing. This type of nonsense.

When the pastor's black Cadillac with its shiny chrome wheels pulled into the parking lot, the faithful cheered. I think he came late on purpose so as to make his grand entrance.

Most people wore blue jeans and sneakers. The pastor showed up in black slacks with a matching jacket. He wore a white shirt and shiny black shoes. Had he come to shoot some hoops or preach a sermon?

As he walked across the parking lot like Denzel on a movie set, our eyes locked. He remembered. He came straight toward me with a laser beam stare. If I had been carrying a gun, I might have reached for it right then. I had seen that stare a million times when I was out on the block doing wrong. He looked like he was going to try to rob me or beat me up.

I stood up from the bench and stood with both feet planted and my hands on my hips. He tilted his head as he got close. Oliver stood up, too.

"What do you want here, sinner?" he asked me.

I gulped. I felt every eye there focus on me.

"Sinner? Who pronounced you God?" I asked the pastor.

Oliver started to say something, but I cut him off.

Some of the men from the church gathered around him, mostly older guys, soft from too much television, dessert, and coffee. I had looked hell in the face on the streets. These guys didn't scare me. Damn, I thought. There are three churches on every block of an Oakland hood. Why did Oliver need to come to this one?

"I'm not God. I'm the pastor, and I..."

Oliver wouldn't be silenced anymore. "This here is my guest, pastor. And I'm afraid I ain't going have you talking to him like that."

Next, he addressed the three men at his side. "And I know y'all ain' trying to intimidate somebody. You might whoop my behind on the chess board, but not one of y'all could last ten seconds in my world. So you best unfold your arms."

It was a standoff. For 30 seconds no one moved. Not a word was uttered. The deacons shot us mad-dog stares. Little girls stopped jumping rope. The birds stopped their singing. The pastor smirked and scowled. "Come on y'all. I'm hungry. Let's say grace and get into this delectable sustenance. What do you say?"

The pastor brushed past us to a grove where the faithful were gathered. They smiled and grinned as he drew close. We lagged behind him and the deacons. He clapped when he got within arms length. It was like Jesus Christ himself had landed on the picnic grounds.

"Let us grab the hand of a neighbor," he commanded. Oliver grabbed my hand. He was still steamed. He squeezed my hand so hard that my fingers hurt. "Owww, man!" I complained.

"Ooops. Sorry, young blood," he whispered.

That made me laugh.

The pastor shot an "I want to blast this nigga" look in my direction. He seemed to be waiting on me to be quiet so that he could begin the prayer. I nodded in his direction and said, "Go ahead and do your thing, boss."

"Let us pray," the preacher said. All heads bowed as if on cue. Everyone closed their eyes, except for me and the little kids. I didn't mean to be irreverent. It's just that I don't close my eyes in a circle of enemies under any circumstances.

"Father," the preacher began. He started off in a slow trot, as though he were shuffling through a dictionary for just the right words.

"God, sometimes…" he grunted.

He paused long enough to gather a loose collection of "Say your prayer preacher" and "Yes, Lord" cries.

"Sometimes, it's so hard, God, when you want to do what is right. We live in a world of darkness. And yet you have called us to be the light. And yet with all the street scum and vermin fighting to get into our churches, we press on, Lord."

Oliver opened his eyes. When his eyes caught mine, we started laughing like two kids.

The preacher continued his monologue.

"...ghetto thugs, Lord. You know the kind...."

I doubled over at the waist.

The woman who had tried to stop me from eating the chicken leg hollered, "Satan, I bind you up in the name of Jesus!"

An elderly man's voice muttered, "Get thee behind me Satan."

The pastor raised his voice as his prayer continued.

"Lord, we've been pestered by the trifling miscreants, the criminals...."

I fell to my knees in laughter. Oliver pointed at me. Tears of glee ran down his face.

Liza shook my hand. She wasn't laughing. She whispered angrily in my ear. "Y'all stop it. Stop it, now. You keep on, they gonna put us out of the church."

I fought to pull myself together and regained my feet. Oliver couldn't stop laughing.

Finally, the preacher said, "Deliver us from this evil, oh God. And bless this food. Let the words of your servant serve as prayer. In Jesus's name. Amen."

When the preacher said "Amen," the hoardes rushed toward the food. Except for me, no one had touched a speck of food. I wondered what would have happened if some last minute call had prevented the preacher from arriving at all to say the grace. Would they have packed up the food, uneaten, and turned around for home? This was too wild for me. I believe in God, but this man was practicing mind control. He had a lot in common with Phenomenal.

After Oliver's laughter had ceased, a quiet rage fell over him. In the streets, respect is everything, and the preacher had disrespected us. At one point in his life, Oliver might have killed for less. Liza made him sit down on a picnic bench. He picked at a tender barbecue rib and nibbled at a chicken leg. He looked at me and then tilted his head back toward the grove where the majority of the church members were sitting. "Let's go," he said. I didn't want to go, but Oliver was my friend so what could I do?

The flock was gathered around the preacher, hanging on his every word as though he was the guest of honor at the Last Supper. There was a universal frown as we approached.

"Reverend, my friend here has a problem," Oliver said.

"If you ask me, he has several problems. He has two black eyes for one." The preacher replied with a twisted smile.

Before the preacher could say something that would have got him smacked across the mouth, Oliver cut him off.

"Reverend, we are God's church, and it's about time we did something about these young girls caught up in the pimp/ho game back down in the flats."

The preacher waved with the back of his hand. "That's ghetto mess. I can't be bothered with that nonsense. I'm not a policeman or a social worker, Oliver."

"But Pastor, I don't think you fully understand."

"I understand you, Oliver. There's nothing wrong with my hearing."

"Some of the girls are kidnap victims. A whole lot of them are nothing more than children. They're nuthin' but babies."

The preacher shoved a generous mouthful of potato salad into his pie hole.

"Oliver, did you make the potato salad?"

"Yes, but Rev…"

"This is about the best potato salad that I have ever eaten!"

"But what about the little girls?"

"Oliver, how do you get just the right mixture of onion and egg to go into the potato?" The pastor pointed his white plastic fork at the plate and then rolled his eyes.

"Damn, the potato salad, Rev!" Oliver shouted.

"But I love it, Oliver," he said smiling broadly.

"Come on, Firstborn," Oliver said, wrinkling his top lip in disgust.

The preacher waved as we stood to leave.

"Oliver, you have a nice day. Will we see you in church tomorrow?" he said with his best cheese-eating grin.

Oliver turned around to face the pastor.

"Yes, I'll be there, and I'm bringing my friend."

"This young man?" the preacher, asked pointing at me and frowning.

"No, I'm bringing this friend with me!" Oliver showed the pastor the back of his fist and then popped up his upraised middle finger. A laugh started in my belly and it would not stop. I doubled over again. My ribs hurt but I couldn't stop.

The preacher had been caught off guard. He gasped, but it didn't take him long to recover. "Yes, well, you bring your friend, Oliver. There's room for both of you in the church."

"Really? Great! Then I'll bring his brother, too!" Oliver raised the middle finger on his other hand and marched off with me behind him, tears of laugher streaming down my face.

CHAPTER
EIGHT

WILLIE PEOPLES AND THAT BUNCH WERE PERCHED IN FRONT OF the black iron gates of Ms. Holmes' apartment building. He eyed the Range Rover with a poison stare as we pulled up to the curb. His pitbull pulled her chain taunt as she strained toward us. The four brothers in the sagging jeans who crowded around him barely glanced up at the car, but there was a whole lot of whispering going on. I had little doubt about the topic of discussion.

Oliver shot a look at them and asked, "You all right from here, young blood, or you need me to clear the block?"

I'd be all right, I assured him. I'd have to be all right. Oliver already had a strike, and he was on parole. I didn't want him to get mixed up in something stupid that could get him shipped to Soledad State Prison, forever.

"No, I'm good OG," I lied. Suddenly, I thought about the exchange between him and the preacher. I burst out laughing again. He laughed, too. Liza was angry at both of us. "Get out of the car, Firstborn. I had enough of you and Oliver both for today. Half a minute more and I'll be putting him out with you," she said.

"You going to church tomorrow?" Oliver asked.

"I'll call you," I answered.

As soon as they drove off, I began to miss Oliver and Liza. I could have stayed at Oliver's house, but I wouldn't have felt right about it. I wasn't back in Oakland on a social visit. Willie's evil frown reminded me of that. I would have to deal with him. He and his goons were blocking the gate. Damn.

"Good evening, gentlemen," I said sarcastically.

Willie Peoples got a little closer to me than I felt comfortable with. He stared into my eyes and squinted as though he were looking at the sun.

"You down with dem Black Christmas niggas ain't you?"

I shook my head vigorously. "I'm a college student and I'm down with the books."

Willie yanked the lit cigarette from his lips and held it between his forefingers. He pointed the fire end at me. He squinted at me and then whispered, "You a lie. You down with Drama. You his number one boy. They tell me you the one Sideshow Psycho was talkin' 'bout in that song, '…Firstborn is the capo, the number two nigga/The one who can get you done with the trigger….'"

I coughed into my hand. "Yeah, well that was a long time ago. I don't even live in Oakland anymore."

Willie Peoples spit on the ground. "Listen lame, Ms. Holmes good people. She and my mama is friends. And you got a pass cause you with her. But I hate them Black Christmas niggas, and if they come round here with that get down or lay down speech they been handin' out all over the Town, then it's on. 'Cause we ain't layin' down and you ain't extortin' us. And when the funk jump off, you'll be the first to get it, feel me? I got something for you and Drama."

A short boy with bulging eyes pulled up his shirt. He nodded as I looked at the butt of his semi-automatic. "That's a 16 clip fulla real talk. Feel me?"

I nodded. "Like I said, I'm not down with any of that now. I'm a college student."

The crew parted and I went through the front doors. It was easy to die in East Oakland. The streets will swallow you up before you blink. I had seen it happen to a lot of brothers I knew. I didn't want it to be me. I'd been lucky so far. Maybe it was time to go back to San Jose. I was sorry for Crayon, but what the hell else could I do?

Before I could knock on the apartment door, it swung open. "Where you been? She called!" Ms. Holmes said in a single breath.

I was surprised and curious. "What did Crayon want?" I quizzed.

"She wouldn't tell me. She said to tell you to call her. The number's on the refrigerator."

I whipped out my cell and walked through the kitchen. Someone had scrawled a phone number on a paper napkin. I pressed the numbers and held my breath. I became aware of my heart's jackhammer thumping in the anxious moment before the phone was answered.

"Hello."

"Yeah, whassup? This is Firstborn."

"Firstborn?"

"Uh-huh."

"I'm pregnant."

I could hear Sapphire in the background. "C'mon, girl. They coming back any minute. Your arm ain' broke. Hang up that phone and let's go."

"Crayon, what's going on?"

"I'm pregnant, Firstborn. When I told Phee, he told me I wasn't having it. He said, 'Babies is bad for business.' I told him I was having my baby. That's when he started twisting my arm. It was like he was trying to rip it out the socket. It hurts."

"Where are you, Crayon?"

She was silent. Sapphire was shouting, "Come on girl. We got to get up out of here."

"He'll kill you, Firstborn," Crayon stated crisply.

"I'll take my chances. Let me come down there to get you."

She sighed. "We'll be in the sandwich shop on Broadway and 12th, but hurry. And don't bring my grandmother."

I hung up the phone and turned to Ms. Holmes, who was at my elbow, pie-eyed and hungry for news about the conversation.

"Ms. Holmes, I need to borrow your car."

"For what?"

"You gonna have to trust me."

"Trust you?" She said it like I was asking her to believe in little green Martians. "I been trusting you to bring my grandchild back home, and you ain't done nothin'. My car ain't going nowhere without me in it," she said.

Ms. Holmes went into her bedroom and emerged two minutes later with an overcoat and a pair of bedroom slippers. In a flash, she was back in the kitchen. She rustled through a kitchen drawer and extracted a 10" meat cleaver. "Here, take this," she said. I was left to look at her back as she rushed out the door. I tucked the meat cleaver in my belt band and then started out after her. As old as she was, I could barely keep up with her.

Ms. Holmes pushed an ancient brown Chevy Impala. As soon as I told her where Crayon was, she slammed the pedal to the floor. The speedometer only went up to 80, and she was doing every mile of it. We hit the 580 freeway like a bullet. Ms.

Holmes was weaving in and out of traffic, never slowing. Car horns blared. People blinked their lights at us.

Ms. Holmes ignored them. She could only see her baby.

When the Impala got close to our destination, I hollered, "Wait here!" and jumped out.

I raced into the restaurant – two minutes too late. Crayon was there, but she was not alone. She sat in a booth with her back to the door. She was resting her head in her hands. She screamed, "I ain't got no money. He got it all. I told you that trick robbed me."

Phenomenal reared back to slap her, but I grabbed his arm.

"Don't even think about it, punk!" I hissed.

I could tell, Phenomenal wasn't used to people telling him, no. He snatched his hand away.

"Damn, potna, this between me and my woman. You all up in my Kool-Aid."

Before he could finish cussing me out, the glass doors blew open. The man who walked in was a force of nature. He looked like the African American version of the Incredible Hulk. We didn't need an introduction. His reputation had long preceded him. This was the notorious Black Hole.

The restaurant's owner, a mousey looking man with a thick black mustache, jetted toward the back room. I prayed that he was calling the police.

"What's up?" the giant asked his brother. There was a baseball-sized tattoo on Black Hole's right bicep that said, "Mom." He looked like a mountain walking on bowling pins. Where did he find shirts that fit, I wondered.

Phenomenal called me every foul name he could think of, and then he told his brother that I was coming around messing with his whore.

"Nah, he ain't!" Black Hole growled. He pushed my shoulder. I almost fell. "Nigga, I'm fittin' to work you," he announced.

Black Hole slipped his belt through the loops. Next he snapped it on the floor like a whip. Phenomenal had the doorway blocked, so I ran to the back of the store. "Call the cops!" I hollered at the owner.

He hollered back, "Me no want no trouble!"

Black Hole snapped the belt again as he inched toward me.

"Come here, Crayon," Phenomenal said. She obeyed, backing toward the front door. Black Hole shuffled toward me like a matador closing in a bull. His brother stood behind him, urging him on. "Get him. Get him," he said through gritted teeth.

I snatched open the soda cabinet and picked up a bottle of Peach Snapple, which I lobbed at Black Hole like it was a grenade. He sidestepped it and grinned. Well, he couldn't duck the whole case, I reasoned. I reached back in and grabbed a Mango Madness and then the lemon ice tea. Bottles crashed at his feet. Black Hole stopped his forward motion to cover his face with his forearms. A can of Diet Coke hit him in the head. The giant lurched forward.

He grabbed me with a hand so big that it fit almost all the way around my bicep. He cursed me and then promised to stomp me into a mud hole. I reached beneath my shirt for the meat cleaver. Black Hole was going to have to bring some to get some. Before he could see it coming, I had sliced his arm all the way down to the white meat. He screamed. Blood was spurting everywhere."

"Drop the belt or the next one is going through your windpipe!" I promised. "I've had all the ass whuppings I plan to take, thank you." The belt sounded like a sack of grapefruit when it hit the floor.

"Now me and little Crayon here are walking out of here. Come on, Crayon," I said. But it was too late.

The proprietor came out of the back room and shook his head.

My heart sank. "Is she…?"

"They left, mister."

I looked down at Black Hole, who writhed on the floor in agony.

"Where did they go, big man?" I asked.

He smirked through his pain. "Like I would tell you!"

I wound up like Pele and kicked him in the small of the back. Black Hole shuddered, holding his bloody arm. I took my eyes away from him for a single moment. That was all it took. Black Hole seized my ankle and scrambled to his feet. He lifted me up in the air. I was upside down. The meat cleaver slipped from my fingers and hit the floor with a clang.

My head dangled as he shook me, cursing. He swung me against a wall. I hit with a loud thud. I grunted as the pain shot down my spine. I whirled and gyrated, suspended in mid-air. He raised me up another foot and then punched me in the mid-section. His fist was the size of a football. Uppercuts rained on my kidneys. I could no longer feel my legs. It was a pleasure when he dropped me. His blood was everywhere. It covered my shirt. I could feel dampness on my cheek and chin. I lay on the floor. Black Hole scooped up the meat cleaver. "Let me see this," he said to himself.

The front door opened. An elderly white couple started to enter. All of our eyes met at once. The gentleman said, "Pardon me." He backed out of the door bowing and saying, "Excuse us."

The first kick stabbed the back of my head. It almost broke my neck. The second one landed between my shoulder blades. The giant lifted up his size 16 shoe to stomp me. I twisted away at the last second before it could land. That was a move I had learned from watching wrestling on television.

Black Hole hoisted the meat cleaver up in the air. But before he could bring it down on my chest, I heard the owner's voice. "Me no want no trouble." This time there was some bass in it. We both turned to look at him. He was toting a .44 Magnum. The business end was leveled at Black Hole's Adam's apple. "Le' him go."

Black Hole stepped back, silent as I limped quickly for the front door.

Ms. Holmes was double-parked by the curb, frantically beating on the car horn. When I snatched open the car door, she hollered, "I saw them. He took her. He threw her in the back of a truck and took off. What was you doing in there, eating a sandwich? She gone. She gone."

I collapsed in the seat next to Ms. Holmes. I was breathing hard and covered in blood. She shot me an angry glance and clicked her dentures.

CHAPTER
NINE

THE RIDE BACK TO EAST OAKLAND WAS A QUIET ONE. WILLIE Peoples and his crew were raising hell elsewhere, so we were able to move into the building unmolested. The hallway seemed dark, narrower. The whine of sirens drew close, and then they sped away.

Bob Marley's "Concrete Jungle" thundered from behind someone's door. Rakim's 16 bars sounded like the soundtrack to the ghetto.

The apartment door opened with a creak I had never heard before. Ms. Holmes had yet to say a word. She shuffled into the apartment, head bowed. She draped her coat over a chair and then put a pot of coffee on the stove.

"I guess you'll be heading back to San Jose tomorrow," Ms. Holmes said in resignation. I could tell that she had made up her mind that I would never be able to get her granddaughter back. I could see how someone could come to that conclusion. Phenomenal and his crew would be looking for me after what I did to his brother. I could expect to be murdered if I stayed around Oakland, and it would be a surprise if it turned out any other way.

I told Ms. Holmes that I wanted to take a good long soak in the tub. I wanted to soak the ache out of my muscles. I wanted to wash Black Hole's blood off my body. I felt like walking death.

Yes, it was all over. I had tried my best. Now it was time to think about saving myself. I took a nice, long, hot bath, and then I walked into Maggie's room and closed the door. I slipped on my pajamas and laid down on top of the sheets. The adrenaline rush would not let me rest. I lay trembling in the darkness, staring out the window at East Oakland. Where was Crayon? Was she really pregnant? Was she afraid? Was her arm really broken?

It was almost 10:00 p.m. by now. I could hear Ms. Holmes rummaging around in the kitchen. I traced her footsteps as they shuffled back and forth from room to room. She must have thought I was asleep. She opened the door to the room and just stared at my prone frame in the darkness. She shook her head and then said something that sounded like profanity, though I couldn't be sure. The door closed and the footsteps continued. Soon, I heard an ungodly wail. She tried to catch her breath after it was released. Ms. Holmes hollered, "Jesus! Jesus! Jesus!"

I sat up and placed both feet on the floor. I wanted to go into the living room to comfort her, but did I dare? The one who had caused her so much pain and heartache? I let her cry. It seemed as though she would never stop. Her voice soon grew raw and ragged from the moaning and sobbing.

It was then that I made my decision. I'm not proud of it. And if you wanted to put this book down and not even read the rest of this, I wouldn't blame you. Because I promise you it will get ugly.

I reached into my wallet and pulled out the business card War Thug had given me – the one that said, "Situations Handled." The phone rang twice, and then a woman's voice answered. I recognized it immediately. It was Mamacide. The last time I had seen her, she was pointing the business end of a Mossberg shotty at my eyebrow line.

"Whass up?" she drawled while popping bubble gum.

I didn't want to waste words speaking with her. Maybe she wouldn't recognize my voice.

"Put Drama on the phone," I demanded.

"Firstborn, my nicca," she said cackling. "Whass poppin' baby? We ain't heard from you in a minute. Glad you still alive, homie."

"Put Drama on the phone," I repeated.

"Drama don' talk on no phones."

"How can I get up with him?"

"Give me a number," she said. I gave it to her, and then the phone went dead.

Five minutes later it rang.

"His cousin, Sideshow Psycho, gon' be in the studio tomorrow afternoon. You know that place on Adeline?"

"I remember the place."

"Be there at noon, sharp."

She hung up without another word.

"AT THAT MOMENT IT WAS LIKE I HAD NEVER LEFT EAST OAKLAND."

CHAPTER
TEN

THE NEXT DAY WAS SUNDAY. MY BRUISES WOKE ME UP. I FELT AS though someone had thrown me under a Mack truck. It hurt to even turn over. I called Oliver early and told him I wouldn't be going with him to Greater Grace. I told him I was going to get something to eat and might take in a movie later. I didn't tell him about what had happened the night before. I also skipped the part about going to see Drama. I already knew he would disapprove of that, and I didn't feel like arguing, not on that particular morning.

I went to the bathroom and pissed blood. Damn those kidney punches. I got dressed slowly. Ms. Holmes was seated at the kitchen table staring at the wall. She was still in her housecoat and slippers. This was odd because she never missed church on Sunday.

"I might need to stay on a few more days," I said. She shrugged her shoulders. There was a "nobody's home" look in her eyes. I didn't smell biscuits baking, and no coffee was brewing. It wasn't like her to not offer a meal. I scratched my head, puzzled. She was still in a catatonic state when I started for the door. I asked if she wanted me to bring her back something to eat, but she didn't answer, so I just left.

I walked over to the McDonald's at Eastmont Mall. I ordered a meal and nursed a cup of coffee until about 11:00 a.m. Then I went out to the bus island and caught the first of two buses that would take me over to Adeline Avenue.

I wasn't crazy about Sideshow Psycho. In fact, I thought he was an idiot. He drank heavily and talked too much about things that should never come out of his mouth. They called him Sideshow Psycho because he was a local fixture at the sideshows. That's when we block off the street and swing our cars in a tight circle. In your hood, they might drag race. In our hood, we do the sideshow. It can be fun to see the tires smoke and then tap on the back of the cars as they swing in a circle. It takes skill to do this without bapping somebody else's car. Sideshow Psycho didn't have that skill, and because of that he had dented up a number of cars. But he was Drama's first cousin from New Orleans, so people let it go.

Drama kept Psycho away from the dope game. After he dropped out of school, Drama started paying for his studio time. His cousin loved hip hop, and he was good at it. Drama started a label called BCM recordings and signed Sideshow Psycho as the first act. He was getting some shows and even a little radio play. Drama paid one of the hottest hip hop artists in the Bay a nice piece of money to spit 16 bars on one of Psycho's tracks. The kid was starting to get his name out there. There was a chance that he might blow up one of these days.

When I got to the studio, Sideshow Psycho's girl, Lydia, opened the door. She had huge brown eyes and a lovely shape. She was in her second year of pre-med studies at Allston. She tried to say "hi," but the music was too loud. All she could do was beckon me in.

A skinny, white cat in a Led Zeppelin T-shirt hunkered down over the soundboard, pushing buttons on the digital console. He nodded his head to the slap beats slamming out of the monstrous overhead speakers. It sounded like Sideshow Psycho was rhyming in a basketball arena. His voice was crisp and clear. "When Black Christmas hit the spot/We ain't leaving without your knot/You know how we get down/We're all niggas talk about in the Town...."

Sideshow Psycho shook his dreads like a mop. A blunt hung out of his mouth. He looked at me and smiled. He was rhyming about things he had heard about, perhaps even seen. If you asked him, he would tell you that he was keeping it real. But in reality, he had never actually done anything he was speaking on. That made me ill because some kid, somewhere, someday might try to emulate a lifestyle that Sideshow Psycho had fabricated in a recording studio. You can't tell me it doesn't happen. I've seen it.

"Damn, that's phat," Sideshow Psycho hollered out over the heavy bass beat.

I shook my head in disgust. "Fool, will you wake up!" I hollered back. "Black Christmas is a criminal organization. Frank Sinatra might have known every made man in the Mafia, but he wasn't making records about them! When those cats walked up in the club, Ol' Blue Eyes might have given them the nod, but he wasn't shining a spotlight down on somebody who did crime for a living, pointing them out for the Federal government, dry snitching."

Sideshow Psycho looked straight ahead of him, his jaws tight, his complexion reddening. "Drama likes it. In fac', he wanna call the next album 'Black Christmas.' He spittin' bars on this next joint. Wanna hear it?"

Before I could shout out the words, "Of course not, you idiot!" the engineer had it cued up.

"I stay wit heat/Niggas got to eat/My brother Firstborn renamed the street/We started with trees/Now we movin' dem keys/I'm stackin' these g's/I got game disease…."

Something got caught in my throat, and I started hacking.

Psycho tilted his head back and laughed. "Need some water, Firstborn?"

"Fool, take me to see Drama!" I finally got out.

Psycho rose from the console. "Eddie, take a break. I'll be back in 20 minutes," he told the engineer. "Baby, wait right here for me," he told his girl.

"C'mon, Firstborn."

He relit the blunt and then walked out of the front door with me in tow. Psycho's car was a classic Pontiac Grand Prix. It had a purple paint job and gold wire wheels. He popped the door locks, and I climbed in. The interior had been beautifully restored; the seats were cotton-soft leather.

Sideshow Psycho pulled away from the curb. The music was on volume 10. The AC was on blast, and he was smoking his herb with the windows up. I was catching a contact buzz just sitting next to him.

"Must you smoke that in here?" I hollered.

"I must," he said laughing.

We took the 580 freeway back to the Fruitvale exit. We flowed through the Murder Dubbs, Funk Town, The Dirty Thirties, Jingle Town, The Rolling Sixties, The Shady Eighties, Brookfield, 11-500, Stone City, and then we came to a stop in the Rolling Hundreds. About then we circled back to our hood.

Sideshow Psycho doubled-parked with the engine running. He pointed at an alley about three houses up. Two brothers in long T-shirts were there, hanging out like they were waiting for somebody. Psycho turned the music down without lifting his hand all the way off the dial. "Welcome home, my nigga," he said. "You got two black eyes, but I don't even want to know 'bout that. I guess that's a Drama conversation."

"You're not getting out?" I asked.

"Hell, no. Drama told me to bring you here, and you're here. So get out my ride and do your thing, playa."

I wasn't new to this turf. I had grown up not too far from here. And I could tell that the city of Oakland had lost legitimate control of the four-block radius around where I was standing. Oh, they'd send the sanitation department out to pick up trash. They'd send the coroner out to pick up bodies, but the law and order part? Forget it. That was clearly over with.

I stopped at the mouth of the alleyway between two three-story apartment buildings. There he was in the courtyard beyond me, seated with his back to the streets. Drama's grandfather, a full-blooded Native American, had passed down a head of straight black hair with a trace of kink in it to his grandson. A brother with two long pigtails sticking out beneath a white Stetson brim is impossible to miss.

This was going to be wild. I wondered how it would go. Drama and I had parted on the worst possible terms. He'd left me stranded in a room full of gangstas that he had just robbed. In all reality, they should have killed me, but they didn't. Drama had been my best friend, and yet he left me there alone. I broke out of Oakland a week after it happened. Drama and I hadn't spoken since that night. My heart skipped a beat. What would happen now?

Wolves, jackals, hyenas, and vampires prowled in broad daylight. There were hitters on the block. I could feel the piranhas swarming. I know what I'm talking about. A year ago, I was out here calling shots in this very hood.

Two loiterers stopped me as I tried to make my way through the alley to where Drama was sitting.

"What you want here, lame?" A stocky boy with gold teeth and a fresh haircut pressed his palm against my chest.

"I'm here to see Drama."

His partner, a thin man with a part in the middle of his head drew close to me. He cocked his head sideways and stared into my eyes, trying to intimidate me. There was a BCM tattoo on his neck. I didn't recognize him. Not that that means anything. I hadn't been around in close to a year. I tried to back up, but they kept circling me, eyeing me up and down. The kid with the part pulled a .007 knife from his waistband. It dangled at his side.

"What you want with a thoroughbred nigga like Drama... officer?" the young fellow asked.

"I'm not the police. Drama is my brother."

The stocky one slapped my front pants pocket with the palm of his hand. The leather wallet inside sounded like a drum. "Your brother? Drama ain' got no brothers."

He slapped the pocket with the wallet inside, again.

The thin one laughed.

"Break it off, lame," the one with the part and the gold teeth hissed. He poked me in the stomach with the blade. When I hesitated, he went in a little deeper. He poked a little hole in my shirt. A tiny droplet of blood stained the tip of the knife.

The thug with the part in his hair wasn't laughing anymore. "Hurry up, about it. You keep playing us, this is going to the next level," he said.

If I yelled and they panicked, I'd be a homicide victim. If I gave them the wallet and they found four dollars and a bus transfer inside, I still might be a homicide victim. Forget it. I'd have to take my chances. I hollered, "Drama!" Instantly, his head flipped around. I waited for the blade to plunge in. He jumped to his feet when he heard my voice. He pointed at the two hoodlums.

"That's my brother! Whatch'all doing back there?" he hollered.

The two jumped back. The murder stare evaporated from their eyes. Fear replaced it. The chubby guy stuck out his hand to be shaken. Was he joking? I brushed past the two of them and headed toward Drama. He sat back in his seat, his back to the alley's mouth.

A few stray streaks of gray peeked out from beneath his godfather brim. Fat diamond squares dangled form both ears. He was smoking the weed he loved so much. He sucked on a long tube with an imitation human skull attached to the end. I walked around the front of him. His black T-shirt read, SILENCE IS GOLDEN – DUCT TAPE IS SILVER. The creases in his black jeans were so sharp they could have stood up by themselves. His Jordans looked like they had just come out of the box. His eyes were shielded by his loc shades. A fat diamond glistened on his pinky finger.

If Drama was seated with his back to the streets, I knew he had somebody watching it. Mamacide sat in a chair about 2 feet away. She held a black tech-9 in her lap. Her forefinger was nestled on the trigger. She nodded when I walked into the courtyard. Homegirl had gone and gotten herself tatted up since I'd last seen her. She looked like she'd been pumping a little iron, too. A tattoo on Mamacide's bicep said, BOSS BITCH. There was a Christmas tree stenciled on her neck. Below it, I read the words: "Paid In Full."

Drama leapt up from the chair. He placed the skull bong down on the concrete. Then, he threw his arms around me. "What's poppin', homie?" he said. I hugged back. It wasn't a warm hug.

"C'mon man, give me a real hug. We brothers ain't we?" Drama asked.

I eyed him coolly. "I don't know. Are we?"

He chuckled. "C'mon cuz, take a walk with me. I got to take care of some business."

Drama said nothing to Mamacide, and she knew better than to ask where we were headed. The two who had tried to rob me stepped back when we hit the mouth of the alley. Drama pointed in their direction and snarled, "I'ma need to talk to y'all a little later."

The chubby one stuttered, "We-we-we ain' know that was your…"

"Yeah, I'm glad he's back for one. There's been a drought on real niggas 'round here lately," Drama said with a steely-eyed stare.

When Drama's foot hit the sidewalk, six foot soldiers fell in line behind us. They were younger cats. I didn't recognize any of them. They followed us without a word. The driver of a brand new red Acura beeped his horn as we crossed at the corner. People waved and tooted at Drama like he was a rock star. He took it in stride, nodding and throwing up the Black Christmas Mob hand sign.

"We got a lot to talk about, Firstborn."

"A whole lot," I added.

"Let me take care of this little bit of business first."

"You don't have any work on you, do you?" I asked. I knew Drama was hot, and I didn't want to go to jail for just walking down the street next to him.

He chuckled and then stuck a toothpick in his mouth. "It ain't like it used to be, cuz. A boss don't touch no work. This here is organized crime. We got six houses and the product is moving day and night. I don't even be out here too tough. I got capos and lieutenants minding the stores. We moving them keys, my nigga. It's like that." Drama snapped his fingers to accentuate his point.

About half a block away, I spotted three young boys in black hoodies loitering on a corner. I knew this was where we were headed. Drama started cursing under his breath, "Young renegade mutha…"

It was clear that these guys were armed, and I didn't see anywhere that Drama could have been carrying a gun. What was he was going to talk about without a .9mm in his hand?

A light-skinned boy with razor cuts in his eyebrows nodded as Drama drew close. He reached his hand in the pouch of his hoodie. He wanted us to know he was strapped. Drama just smiled and said, "What's up?"

The boy with the pistol in his pouch nodded. The other two just stared. They looked young and afraid.

"Y'all know who I am?" Drama asked.

"No," the boy with the gun said. "Should we?"

Drama smiled showing all 32 gold teeth. "My name is Drama." And then he said in a sing-song voice, "If you don't know, you better ask somebody."

Drama rubbed his hands together. "You know this my corner, right?"

A kid who couldn't have been more than 17 said, "We'll move."

"Nah, nah, y'all ain' gotta move. It's too late for that anyhow," Drama said.

"We don't want no trouble, blood," the third kid pleaded.

"You must want some trouble, else you wouldn't be slinging that work in my hood.

Drama had a way of intimidating people. He was all the way inside the young kid's skull, and he hadn't even had to produce a gun. He hadn't raised his voice. He hadn't made any threats. There was something about Drama, call it an aura, that said, "This man is not to be messed with."

"I don't want any trouble," the kid reiterated.

"I don't want no trouble either," Drama countered. "I'm a businessman, not a killer."

Now, that was two lies. Lie one: Drama lived for trouble. That's why everybody called him Drama. And as for the businessman who's not a killer part? Drama was a cold piece of work who would toss somebody's granny in a pool full of great white sharks and then bet two dollars on which shark would be the first to reach her.

The light-skinned boy with the gun had heart. "Y'all don' scare me," he said. "We got guns, too."

Drama sucked his teeth, annoyed. The toothpick between his lips did a dance. He asked for my cell phone. I obliged. He hit a number. He stared impatiently at the kid as the phone rang. Drama's pupils transformed into stainless-steel balls. He whispered into the phone, grinding his teeth between sentences.

"Yeah, come through," he said. Then, he turned back to the youngster. "Let me show you what I'm working with."

Instantly, a bored-out Hemi engine roared to life just beyond sight. Car tires squealed. A black '77 Firebird raced up the block and made a quick 180-degree turn in the middle of the block, screeching to a stop in front of them. The smoked back window on the passenger's side slid down. The business hole of an AK-47 rested on the window ledge as it pointed straight at the young man's throat. His jaw dropped.

Two familiar eyes stared out at us. The narrow slits of hate barely opened up to let in the sunlight. "Yeah, nigga, now whass up?" I could hear Petey's muffled voice from beneath the black bandana that covered the bottom half of his face. He glanced at me, and in a much friendlier tone, he said, "Firstborn, you done come home! What's really good, my nigga?"

I saluted in Petey's direction. I had put Petey on. He was a stone killer.

I had respect for the light-skinned kid. He had heart, either that or he was 51/50. "You ain' gon' punk us. This ain't even Black Christmas Mob turf," he said.

Drama smiled, "Ahhh,…so you do know who we are. Black Christmas turf is wherever I happen to be standing, fool. But you're lucky because we got a sale on today. We're renting out corners. From now on we're partners. That nigga with the kater aimed at your melon, that's Petey. He's going to collect the taxes for us."

"Taxes? How much?" the light-skinned kid asked.

"Drama named a very exorbitant figure.

"Yo, man there ain't even that kind of money out here like that," he said.

Drama wasn't in the mood to negotiate. "Get down or lay down!" he said.

The kid took a look at the merciless, gray eyes that peered over the top of the black bandana. I could see his will melt. Drama began to walk away. I followed him. I thought the whole confrontation was over, but apparently not, because before the kid could walk away, Petey cried out: "Hold it a minute! Break yo' self nigga!"

The young man's face contorted into a mask of sorrow. "This my rent money," he moaned.

"Well, tell the landlord he won't be gettin' paid this month," Petey said.

The mark turned to Drama, "I thought you said we was partners."

Drama shrugged his shoulders. "Yeah, like a pimp and his ho are partners."

Impatience flexed in Petey's voice. "I'm not gon' say it again, chump. Put the money in Drama's hand. You got that money on Black Christmas Mob turf. That's our money. Now check it in, bitch." The kid hesitated. In a second he would reach for that pistol in his pouch. I thought maybe divine intervention had put me here to save his life. I took a few steps in the direction of the renegade hustlers.

"It's all bad," I said to the kid. "Walk away with your life."

He wasn't quite ready to surrender. "What, y'all think you're the only ones out here with heat?"

My heart raced. Was this young fool going to make a stand with an AK-47 pointed at his Adam's apple.

"I know you're brave brother, but this ain't your day. I'm telling you, I know these cats."

"Yeah, you should. You're one of 'em, Firstborn." He scowled. I felt my heart sink when he called my name. Yet he listened to reason. The brothers all pulled knots of money from their pockets and slipped them into Drama's outstretched hand.

"Smart niggas..." Drama said as he turned on his heel and walked away.

Drama never looked back, but I did. Pure, unadulterated hatred rushed out to meet me from the dealer's pupils. I knew that if Drama ever slipped, those young boys would kill him...and me, too. And I told him so.

"You livin' too fast Drama, I commented. "Ain' everybody gon lay back while you punk 'em with that AK. This is Oakland. Sooner or later, you're gonna run up on some real live Town thugs. And they won't want to get down or lay, then what're you gonna do?"

I might as well have been speaking to the wind. He ignored me.

Mamacide pulled up in a late-model, white Buick Lacrosse. War Thug's smiling face poked out from the back seat. Drama tugged gently at the crook of my arm. "Let's roll, blood. We outta here."

I hopped in the back seat next to War Thug. He reached over and embraced me. He looked at my two black eyes and sucked his teeth. Sideshow Psycho's new song, "Last Stand," was blasting through the speakers. "...I can't change my ways/I'm going out in a blaze/ Bussin' my 9 /Smokin' purple haze...."

At that moment, it was like I had never left East Oakland.

"THE ANGELS WERE ON HIS SIDE THAT AFTERNOON. HE'D COME HALF AN INCH FROM BEING KILLED."

CHAPTER
ELEVEN

"Where we goin', baby?" Mamacide asked as we cut past Foothill and 105th Avenue.

"Just drive," Drama growled.

I could feel sweat dripping off my palms. War Thug poured purple weed into a Swisher Sweet cigar leaf. Tension filled the insides of the vehicle. The conversation I had dreaded was about to begin.

"You crossed some major game, my nigga," Drama said. He didn't turn around to face me. I was looking at his ponytail, forced to talk to the back of his head.

"Drama, you were wilding out. I couldn't let you just kill Latin Caesar like that. Plus, you had it all wrong. He wasn't gonna blast us. He was willing to work with us so we could get his money back."

Drama raised his middle finger. "This is for Caesar," he said.

"Now that's crude," I responded.

Drama ignored me. "Firstborn, when I put you on I told you the rules of the game. And when things get a little hot, you gon' act like a scared little…"

I felt myself getting hot. I sat up. "Hold on a minute, there champ. And turn around when I'm talking to you!"

War Thug's jaw dropped. I'm sure no one ever talked to Drama like that. They were all too afraid. The thing was that no one had ever been closer to Drama than me. And I was angry now.

"You act like I got on a witness stand and turned you," I said. "Negro, I stopped you from committing a homicide. For all you know, I saved every one of you a trip to the gas chamber. Instead of trying to check me, you should be thanking me."

There was an electric silence in the car. I had taken them all off guard. They had never thought of it the way I said it. I had spoken the truth. And that's one thing most people in the streets recognize and appreciate – the truth. Drama pulled a blunt from behind his ear and lit the tip of it with a silver lighter. That meant he was beginning to relax.

"Hey, Firstborn, why did you come back to the East?" he asked.

I took a deep breath and started with Ms. Holmes' visit. I told him about Crayon and about my frustration. The truth was, if Drama didn't help me, there was no way I'd be able to get Crayon out of the Life. And I told him so.

"I wish I could help you, homie. But we don't do no non-profit work. If it don't make dollars, it don't make sense. That's how we doing it now," Drama said.

I couldn't believe my ears. "'...wish I could help you, homie?'" I said. "'Black Christmas Mob fo' life!'" And 'anything for my brothers!' Ain't that what you used to say?"

Drama turned around to face me. "That's what I still say."

I pulled my last card. This one came from the bottom of the deck. "You aren't afraid are you, Drama?"

"What!" he hollered.

"Well, I know that Phenomenal and his team are pushing a real line. I been hearing a lot about him and his brother, Black Hole, in these streets. Maybe you don't have it like that anymore. Maybe all of this money has made you a little soft. I can't blame you though. You don't…"

War Thug broke his silence. I could feel his spit on the bridge of my nose as he spoke. "Nigga, are you out your mind? Who you think you talking to? That's taking it a bit far even for you. That pimp must have knocked some brain cells loose."

Drama smiled. But it was not a happy smile. It was the kind of smile he flashed before someone got their dome split open. "Yeah, I heard Phee was saying something about Chopper. What was it?"

I repeated all the vile things Phenomenal had called our homie, Chopper. Drama looked out the window and shook his head. I couldn't see his face. We rode in silence. He made no further comment on Chopper. Finally, he changed the subject. "Firstborn, you must be hungry for something you can't get up in San Jo'. Let's get our eat on. Where you wanna go?"

"El Tacqueria," I said.

"What the…?" War Thug asked.

"Nigga, you is crazy!" Mamacide chimed in.

"What's wrong? We used to eat there all the time," I said.

I knew exactly what was wrong. What I neglected to add (but didn't have to because I knew they all remembered) was that we used to go there with Latin Caesar before it all went bad. Death was just a short walk from El Tacqueria.

"You got some stuff with you, Firstborn," Drama growled.

"You asked me what I wanted and I told you. I want a burrito from El Tacqueria. You aren't afraid are you, D?"

The car crew quiet. "Mamacide, let's go," Drama said. War Thug pulled his nine out from his hoodie pouch. He slapped a fresh clip in the butt and then tucked it underneath the oversized sweater. War Thug stared out the window as the neighborhoods changed.

"Yeah, I'd like a burritto," I mused to myself.

Drama had put me in the car to straighten me out. But I had turned the tables on him. I had him. I told you I knew the man.

Oakland isn't like Detroit or Chicago. It's a small city, which means that if you get into something in these streets, trouble is never far from you. Ten minutes from the moment, the decision was made to eat at El Tacqueria, we were pulling into the parking lot. War Thug looked at me and shook his head like I was a lost cause. He tucked his banger in his hoodie pouch and never removed his hand from it.

Drama opened the car door and stepped down on the pavement like an astronaut setting foot on the moon. His eyes flipped in every direction, appearing just a little unsure of himself. He sauntered toward the front door of the restaurant with Mamacide in tow. War Thug and I followed closely behind.

At the counter, Drama looked back and asked, "What y'all want?"

I asked for a steak burrito and two soft-shell chicken tacos. I got a large Coke with that. Drama paid.

I looked at Mamacide and War Thug and asked, "Aren't y'all gonna eat?"

They seemed preoccupied. War Thug was hunting for all the exits. Mamacide picked her nails and cussed under her breath.

"I ain't hungry," War Thug said. "Me neither," agreed Mamacide.

"Sure, y'all get something to eat," I said. "I hate eating alone. And how often do we get to see each other? And shoot, Drama's treatin'."

War Thug was so shocked by my raw nerve that he let out a genuine laugh. "Nigga, you are out of your natural mind," he said.

"Still, get something to eat," I said.

A short man with a thick mustache and jowls took our order. He pointed at two tables and asked us to sit. We were the only people in the store who weren't of Mexican descent. Mariachi music floated from the speakers. Drama put his arm around Mamacide. She reveled in the moment, smiling broadly. "So tell us about college, Firstborn," Drama said.

"Well, I write for the school newspaper. I sing in the glee club. I'm a journalism major. I have three roommates. Each of them is younger than me, and they drive me up the wall. I'm getting great grades. You know I'm a transfer student, and I'll have my bachelor's degree in less than two years," I said.

"And?" he asked, spreading his hands.

"And what?" I asked.

"Is there a nice young lady out there for you?

"Oh, yes. I've met a fine chick up there. Her name is Caitlin."

Before I could go on any further, the man with the mustache brought out a tray with our food on it. Drama had ordered Cokes for the rest of the crew. I dug in.

About halfway through my burrito, a dude sporting gang colors walked through the front door. He stared at us for just a millisecond. His eyes squeezed together. In an instant, he turned around and walked back out the door, never looking at us again. We watched him cross the street. When he hit the corner he wasn't walking – he was jogging.

"Let's be out!" War Thug hollered.

I waved at the waiter. "Can I have a to-go bag," I asked.

"Nigga, is you stupid?" Mamacide inquired. "We got to get up out of here now!"

We raced back to the car. Mamacide turned the key in the ignition. We were in and ready to roll before the engine could turn over.

"What are you so afraid of?" I asked, laughing.

The Buick zoomed out of the parking lot and into traffic.

We pulled up to a red light at 35th and International Boulevard. I was still giggling when a black 1970 Nova pulled up next to us. My heart stopped. My tongue stuck to the roof of my mouth. I tried to scream, but fear froze my vocal chords. A pair of fiery black eyes stared out over the bandana covering the bottom of a hidden face. The business end of a .380 was aimed right at Drama's head. Finally, I was able to get the name out of my mouth.

"Caesar!"

Mamacide's foot slammed down on the accelerator. The traffic signal in front of us turned red.

"Take the light!" Drama ordered. We zoomed through traffic. Latin Caesar didn't slow down an inch. The Nova was right on our tailpipe.

"Stay down!" Mamacide hollered out.

Just then I heard a gunshot. The back window exploded, showering us with glass.

War Thug came up firing. He couldn't get off a clean shot because Mamacide was weaving in and out of traffic in a desperate attempt to shake them. It was fruitless. The Nova was built for occasions like this. Its engine roared as they overtook us. Our only hope was to get back to our hood. The Deep East was still 30 blocks away.

"Go! Go!" Drama hollered.

Mamacide rolled up on a sidewalk doing 80. People scattered and screamed. The Nova never slowed. I heard a loud ping. A bullet had shattered the side window.

We hit 61st and International Boulevard. "Oh, God, just let us get back to 81st Avenue," I prayed out loud. I felt that they wouldn't follow us that far.

Drama was taking no chances. He rifled through Mamacide's purse for a cell phone.

"This yo nigga, D," Drama screamed into the cell. They on us!" he screamed into the cell.

There was a moment of silence.

"...Yeah, it's dem fools. They're in a black Nova."

Silence.

"Yeah, yeah…. We in the Buick. They done shot out the back window. My nigga, we gonna be to you in like two minutes. Get on it."

Mamacide turned right onto Plymouth Avenue. The Nova was on our bumper, and they were still shooting. Mamacide was driving with her head down in the steering wheel. I had to give it to her. She could wheel. If anybody else had been driving, we'd all have been dead.

They tried to cut around us to the right. Mamacide cut them off. They tried to go left. She cut left. And then we reached the hood.

The phone rang once and then stopped.

"Duck! Duck!" Drama hollered.

Then all hell broke loose. Rifle bullets rained down from rooftops. Machine gun slugs spit from second-story windows. The Nova's front tires were shot out. It skidded into a parked Ford van. The side windows shattered. Somebody I couldn't see was hollering, "Black Christmas Mob fo' life!"

The gangstas in the Nova struggled to turn around in the middle of a one-way street on four flat tires. And then I heard the sirens. We were out of there. Drama was ecstatic. I was pretty happy myself. "Who is king of these streets?" Drama asked. "DRAMA!" Mamacide and I said in unison. When Drama didn't hear War Thug's voice in the chorus he flipped around.

"Thug hit!" he said, shock registering in his voice.

I couldn't believe it. I was sitting right next to him and hadn't realized he'd been hurt. Blood spurted from War

Thug's neck. Drama cursed. "We gotta get him to a hospital," he said.

War Thug sat up. "No, I'm cool. It's a flesh wound. It looks worse than it is. Get me some gauze and alcohol, and I'll be all right."

The angels were on his side that afternoon. He'd come half an inch from being killed.

I was ready for this day to be over.

The car was a crack rental. Drama had traded a smoker the use of his car for a small amount of drugs. Of course, the addict hadn't expected his car to be used as a tank in a war. He'd be surprised. Of that, I was sure.

War Thug, Drama, and I got out at 90th and Avenue D. Mamacide took the car to a garage about a block away. After dark they would take it out near the airport and burn it.

As we stood on the curb trying to catch our collective breath, Drama asked, "That was an expensive lunch. Is there anything else you want?"

"Yes," I said. "I didn't get to have dessert."

CHAPTER
TWELVE

Tiny deflated black balloons littered the sidewalk that led to my destination. My eyes were trained on the arm of the man who opened the door to Fred's Chicken Barn. Small black dots lined his right arm. It was a mess of abscesses and collapsed veins. He wiped his nose with his sleeve and then wiped his brow with a wrinkled black scarf. I followed him. He walked straight toward the bathroom in the rear of the greasy spoon. They're selling dope out of here now, I thought to myself.

It was dark inside even though out in the streets it was high noon. Burned out lightbulbs dangled naked from the ceiling like tiny glass skulls. Virus was the first one I spotted. He sat in a corner with his eyes trained on the front door. Five-foot-three with a sea of trained black waves brushed into his scalp, Virus had been named Russell by his mother. However, in school his behavior was so erratic that the teachers started referring to him as "Violent Russell." The homies switched it up and just started calling him Virus, for short.

The name stuck, and for good reason. Virus owned the baby face of a lead tenor in a boy's choir, but he was not to be slept on. If you walked through that door and just stared at Drama a bit too hard or too long, the next thing you know you'd be shaking hands with Jesus.

Virus waved me over with one hand. The other hand held the .9mm pistol that sat in his lap cocked back with the safety off.

Fred's Fried Fish House was the center of the movement. This is where Drama came to break bread with murderers and to plot hits on rivals. This is where you got yourself a brand new Desert Eagle straight out of the box. A hustler might come down here looking for the player price on a kilo. And it looked like Drama was moving heroin out of the back.

Drama never touched anything. He had goons and flunkies to do all that. The chances people would take to be "down...."

As soon as I sat down, a young brother I'd never seen before strolled up to our table. He sat down and pulled an envelope from the pocket of his jeans. He slid it to Drama underneath the table. Drama gave him a nod. They never exchanged a single word. The kid leaned over and whispered something in Petey's ear. Petey whispered a sentence back. Then the kid just got up and walked out. As soon as he hit the door, Drama looked down and started counting. He took out a hundred from the thick stack and flipped it at Petey. He put three hundreds in my hand and said, "Boss, get yourself some decent fits if you gonna be around me." He stuck the rest in his pocket.

Ricky and Bobby pointed at me as they entered the door. "Firstborn, ain't seen you in a minute, homie. Welcome home, my nigga!"

I smiled and nodded.

Ricky and Bobby were bank robbers. Everybody and his mama knew that. They were guest starring in TV news video clips and "wanted posters" all over the Bay Area. Yet, they always seemed to be broke. Can you imagine somebody who's hitting banks asking something like, "Let me hold five dollars, homie," or "Can you buy me a cheeseburger, Firstborn?"

Back when I was grinding on the turf, I told Ricky, "Bruh, if you can't make any money doing what you're doing, you're better off trying to get a square job."

Bank robbery's a dangerous sport. It's nothing like what you see in the movies. They aren't going to let you walk in the back and load millions of dollars into two or three duffel bags. Hell, no! More than likely, you get a few grand, and then you're on the run, looking over your right shoulder forever. You're facing Federal years for a crime that hardly netted you enough to buy a good set of rims. And the Feds never forget, and they never get tired of hunting you.

The stick-up game had run Ricky and Bobby ragged, and they were ready to switch it up. Petey stuck his hand in his shirt pocket. He plucked out a brass key and then placed it flat on the tabletop. Ricky reached in his pocket and pulled out a wad of bills. He counted out $200 and then slipped it into Petey's hands. In return, Petey slid him the key.

"That's the pass key for every apartment in the building," he said. "Be smart. Don't hit every crib the first day. They don't know who has the key or even that it's missing. If you do this right, you'll be eating for a long time. If you mess it up, they'll change all the locks overnight, and you'll be back stuck on broke. Now like I said over the phone, $200 is a down payment. We expecting the rest before Christmas, dammit. Don't make me have to come looking for y'all."

Petey stared at them through that long nest of dreadlocks. No threats needed. That deadly gaze said it all. These guys were not a solid risk, but it's hard to say no to the guys you came up with. Drama shook his head slowly. His eyes seemed to say, "Niggas never learn."

I tilted my head at Chalet, a notorious dope fiend from the block. She was making her way to the bathroom. "A little business expansion?" I asked.

Drama smiled. I knew him so well I could write a book about each expression. That smile said, "We got to get it how we can get it. That's the game."

Groupies sipped Cokes three tables down. They were the pretty and the lost – mesmerized by the block, hypnotized by the game. They were the type who would hide a toaster or a brick for a good dude. These were the type of girls who put money on your books if you wound up in Santa Rita. Drama ignored them. He thought they were stupid and had no respect for them at all. I'd been there for 20 minutes before he cut his glance in their direction. One girl with bright, red lipgloss almost fell out of her chair.

"You all right, playa?" he asked me.

"Not really, man. I need your help," I said.

"I know you ain't gonna to talk to me about that young chick out on the track again."

Before I could get the words out, Ms. Kramer walked up to our table. She was 50, tall and stately with big hoop earrings and dark chocolate skin. Her eyes were swollen with tears. Drama nodded at the empty chair. Ms. Kramer took the cue and sat. She fished in her pocketbook and pulled out a slip of paper with a phone number written on it.

"What's up, Ms. Kramer?" Drama asked.

"Drama, it's my son, Lolli."

"What's up with Lolli?"

"'Bout three months ago, he was riding down MLK with John when the po po pulled him over. They tossed the car. They didn't have a warrant. They said they had probable cause because they smelled weed in the car. They found a banger underneath John's seat. They said there was prints on it. Now they're trying to tie my boy to armed robbery. Now, my son ain't no angel by anybody's standards, but he would never hurt a fly. That was John's gun, and he won't own up to it."

There are a lot of people in Oakland named John. However, during this particular conversation there was no doubt as to which John she was referring. John was a hard hitter from another hood. He was one of Drama's peers. They had a grudging respect for each other. More than likely, the gun was John's. He probably had priors and warrants and didn't want to add a gun charge to all of that. But Lolli was our homie. John had crossed a line.

Drama looked down at the slip of paper. "Whose number is this?"

"John got a cell phone."

Of course, it was illegal to have a private phone in the house of bars and tears, but a whole lot of brothers with money had them. Drama slid the paper to Petey. He leaned over and whispered something in Petey's ear that I couldn't hear. Petey then asked for Betty's cell phone. She handed it over. Petey dialed the number. We leaned in, listening closely to Petey's end of the conversation.

"John, whass crackin', blood?" This yo' nigga Pete Dawg from the Deep East…. Yeah, that Petey. That's right. Lissen John, who in there with you?"

Petey was silent for a long time as we listened to the rundown of everybody from our hood that was behind bars. It took awhile. It was quite a list. We had a lot of soldiers trapped behind enemy lines.

"Well, look here, man. I'm calling on behalf of my man here. And I'ma make this short. It's about your case. John, you gotta own that gun man. Let Lolli walk."

I could hear a string of raw profanity leap from the phone when Petey yanked it away from his ear.

John didn't want to comply. Petey stuck his finger up in the air as he waited to make a point. His mouth formed a silent O. Finally, there was a break in John's monologue.

"You don't want me speakin' on your case? Personal business? Nigga, you must be on drugs! Check it, John, I'm just going to keep it real and short with you. I know you got all the time in the world in there, but I got things to do and places to be out here. John, that was your banger. Tomorrow morning, you 'bout to call your public pretender and tell her you fixing to plead on that gun case."

Petey stuck his finger up in the air again. His eyebrows rose as he waited another turn to speak.

"No, I ain' crazy, nigga…well, maybe a little…but I'm telling you what you 'bout to do."

Drama leaned over and whispered in Petey's ear again.

Petey conveyed the message. "My man here say, 'Check yo'self, nigga. I'm giving you a chance. You do what we say or we gon' put two racks on your baseball cap. Nigga, you won't live out the weekend. Where you gon' hide in there? You can't escape this mob, nigga.'"

"Nah, where you get that? We ain' making no threats. We don't operate like that. I'm just telling you that if you don't get down, you will never ride through Oakland again, except in a pine box."

Petey nodded and listened. Drama signaled for Petey to lean over. He whispered something in Petey's ear. Petey nodded and then said into the phone. "I got my man sitting next to me. He say, 'Bow down, nigga.'"

"What do you mean, 'Is that how it is, now?' I didn't make myself clear? Carry your own weight and you may live a long time, but if Lolli's mom don't get a happy phone call from her baby boy tomorrow, nigga, you finished, you washed, and I put that on my mama and all my kids. Have a nice day."

Petey clicked the phone off and handed it back to Ms. Kramer. She still looked worried. Petey flashed one of his very rare smiles. "Don't worry," Petey said. "John gotta talk rough and tough for appearances, but that fool ain' crazy. He know what time it is. He'll do the right thing. Lolli comin' home."

Ms. Kramer leaned over and hugged Drama's neck. Her tears spilled onto his collar. Who else could she have gone to with a problem like this, the police?

As Ms. Kramer flipped on her heels to leave, I licked my lips and prepared to make my plea to Drama. Before I could mention Crayon's name again, Juanita walked in. Her son, Tee Rock had been slaughtered when jackers came through the front door of a Black Christmas Mob crack house blasting tech 9s. Tee Rock was 19 years old at the time of his demise.

Juanita was here to ask for some financial relief. Drama didn't offer her a seat. She sat down anyway. He took a deep breath and then whispered into Petey's ear. Petey made a tent with his fingertips. His dreadlocks fell down over his eyes when he leaned forward.

Drama put his hand up, stopping Juanita in mid-sentence. Petey spoke for Drama. "Damn, baby we know you lost a fallen soldier, but we can't be hitting you off every time you come 'round here with your hand out. We ain't payin' no emotional extortion. We can't do it for you this time."

A tear dropped down her cheek. She didn't give up easily. She directed her comments to Drama, even though Petey was clearly doing all the talking.

"Drama, Tee Rock used to help us pay the rent working for Black Christmas. He was one of your best earners. Now me and his brother Renard gettin' ready to get put out."

Drama sucked his teeth in disgust. "You better tell that lazy Renard to get on his griz-zind. The money train done crashed. The ghetto welfare office is closed."

Rage registered on Juanita's face. Drama twisted his head sideways and squeezed his eyes almost shut. It was a look that said, "Go ahead and say it. I dare you!"

Juanita didn't take him up on it. She just walked out.

Two more heroin addicts squeezed by her as she walked out. I started wondering if anyone came here to Fred's to eat the fried fish or chicken. Drama was obviously trying to keep his game away from prying eyes. He wasn't trying hard enough, and he was obviously stirring up a lot of hate in these streets. I had to speak on it. After all, he was the closest thing I had to a brother.

"Drama, you throwing a lot of weight around in these streets, man. How long do you think you can last?"

He waved the back of his hand.

"Firstborn, you talkin' 'bout John? Shhh…we goin' off on niggas' heads all day down here, ya heard? And if that nigga disrespect me by not doin' what he's told, he goin' be the next one to get it. And I ain' hardly bull skating either. That's all I'ma say on that. Now, about this situation with this cat, Phenomenal. I…"

Again, before I could get a word out of my mouth, we were interrupted. Ned walked through the door. Unlike the other people who had approached us, Ned actually walked into the restaurant for the fish and fries. Drama's eyes grew stormy. He raised his voice. "Get over here, fool!"

Nate was Mamacide's 16-year-old cousin. His head was too large for his rail-thin body, and his jeans didn't quite touch his sneakers. Drama couldn't stand him.

"What up, Drama?" Ned asked with a crap-eating grin.

"Say, Ned, did you tell Mamacide something about me?"

The grin grew up into a laugh. "Tell her what, Drama?"

"Did you tell Mamacide you saw me riding another woman around in my car."

"Oh, that?" Ned giggled into the flat of his hand.

Drama's eyebrows raised, and he rose from his seat. He kicked his chair and started toward Ned. Petey stood up, too.

Ned waved his finger back and forth. "Uh-uh, my cousin Mamacide said you wasn't going to lay a hand on me. You ain't going to play my family cheap, Herbert."

That was the ultimate insult. Not only was he talking back, he was giving out Drama's government name. Drama gritted his teeth. His face turned red, but I could see him turning things around in his mind as he grew closer to Ned. Mamacide was a straight savage. There was no telling what she might do if he put his hands on Ned. It was bad business to have a beef with someone you slept with. You might close your eyes one night and never wake up.

"Say," Ned offered, "I have an idea! Why don't you just hit me off with a fifty, and I'll tell my cousin I made a mistake."

Drama's jaw dropped. I'm sure he couldn't believe his ears. Nevertheless, he reached in his pocket and pulled out that fifty. He slammed it into Ned's waiting palm. Ned shot Drama another crap-eating smile and then turned his back. He walked to the counter to order his food. Drama stared a machete through Ned's back but Ned couldn't see it. He shared a joke with the counter man as he ordered his three-piece catfish and fries.

As Drama approached our table again, I tried to get him back on my line. "Drama," I said, "I got this problem. I need your help with man."

He was still staring at Ned. He raised his hand in my direction, signaling for me to put it on ice. Ned received his food and then turned to walk out. He flipped his head toward us, started grinning, and then walked out. That was too much for Drama.

As soon as Ned hit the door, Drama said, "Come on." Petey and I rushed to follow his trot. As Drama had probably guessed, Ned hadn't made it any further than the corner. There he was with four high-school-age cats. He was showing off the fifty-dollar bill, probably talking about where he got it.

I recognized one of them. Li'l Mike had grown about a foot in the year that I had been gone.

"My man, Li'l Mike," Drama said.

Mike sat on his bicycle, shocked that Drama even knew his name. All of his life he had looked at the hood legend from a distance. And now Drama was standing in his breathing space giving him the time of day. Drama grabbed one of Li'l, Mike's handlebars and stared into his face. The kid seemed mesmerized.

"You wanna do a favor for your big homie?"

The young brother didn't even hesitate. "What you need, Drama?"

Drama straightened up and pointed at Ned, a kid Li'l Mike had known since the days of tag and hop scotch.

"He got fifty dollars belongs to me. You get it back, it's yours."

Li'l Mike dismounted from the bike. He passed the handlebars to one of his boys. Fifty dollars is a lot of money in this hood.

Ned's back straightened. His brow wrinkled, "What you trying to do, Drama? That's my money."

Li'l Mike started cracking his knuckles. And then he started in Ned's direction. He was a year older and perhaps a foot taller than Ned. He rolled his head around on his shoulders. Ned looked puzzled. "What you fixing to do, Mike?" he asked.

Mike just continued toward him. When he drew within arm's length he said, "You owe me money. Where my fifty dollars, nigga?"

He was just inches away but still moving closer. "You trippin' nigga. I ain't got none of your money." Ned pushed Li'l Mike's chest.

"Don't touch me, Ned. I'm serious." Li'l Mike folded his bottom lip over his teeth and cocked his head to the side. Ned read the signal.

"Stop trying to crowd me, Mike. What's up?" he said, agitated.

A crowd was beginning to form – old heads and youngsters. You could smell violence in the air. The gathering on the corner grew amped. I could see a smile breaking out on Drama's face as he looked on.

"What's up, Li'l Mike?" Ned asked.

"Fifty dollars is up, nigga. Reach down and bring out a fifty, Ned. Don't make me have to go in your pockets."

Ned glanced to the left and then to the right. He looked lost, confused. Li'l Mike continued to walk in, chest first.

"Mike! Mike!" Ned cried out. He dropped the paper bag with the fish and chips inside.

And then Ned shocked us all. He struck first with a left hook that connected with Li'l Mike's chin. He followed up with a right cross that caused a nosebleed. Li'l Mike drew back, preparing to deliver an overhand right. Ned beat him to the punch, again.

Ned was not to be played with after all. He danced around Mike like he was in a boxing ring. Ned threw a left-right combination that landed on Li'l Mike's nose and lips. The street corner audience howled in shock and delight. Ned was doing more than holding his own. He was beating the hell out of Mike.

Sizing up the situation, Drama signaled to another young man in the crew. They called him Cobra. His baby dreads shook as he jogged over to the hood shot-caller.

"What's up, D?"

"You wanna do a favor for your big homie?"

"Sure. What's up?" he asked.

Drama nodded in the direction of the two combatants and said, "Help out Li'l Mike."

My jaw dropped. "Drama, you foul!" I hollered.

"This ain't Friday Night Fights on ESPN. This is the streets, nigga!" Drama yelled.

That said it all.

Cobra stalked Ned, and when he dropped his hands to hit Li'l Mike again, Ned got his own surprise. Cobra was on him with both hands flying. Sensing help, Li'l Mike grabbed Ned's right leg, yanked it up in the air, and then pushed him backward. Ned struggled to keep his balance, but he fell with both Cobra and Ned on top of him. He tried to get to his feet, but they punished him with lefts and rights. Two sets of fists left him dazed. The three of them were out of breath.

Cobra and Li'l Mike stumbled to their feet. Then, they put the Timberlands to Ned. "Help, help!" he hollered as they took turns stomping and kicking him. Sensing Ned's helplessness, I started forward to break it up before he could be murdered. Drama shook his head and pushed me back. Petey looked me in the eye and shook his head, no.

Ned rolled over moaning. A tear dropped from his right eye. Cobra knelt down. He reached his hand into Li'l Mike's pants pocket and extracted the fifty. He stood up again, waving his prize in the air. The beating stopped. Drama clapped and signaled Li'l Mike and Cobra over. When Drama stuck out his hand, Cobra dropped the bill in it. Drama took the bill and lifted it high. Then, he ripped the fifty in half. He handed one half to Li'l Mike and the other to Cobra.

"From now on, y'all are crew brothers," he said. "The moral of the story is that you earned together; now you eat together. You go get some tape, put that bill back together and agree on how you'll spend it together. Remember, you both earned. You both eat. I'm putting y'all up on some game. Remember it."

Drama took both of their wrists and raised them in the air as if they had they just won the heavyweight title. Then he laughed. "Y'all get up out of here before the pigs come."

Next, he turned his attention back to Ned. The bruised loser was rolling on his back, struggling to find his feet.

There was a deep gash in Ned's forehead. His bottom lip was split. It would need stitches. He had a broken look on his face, the kind you see on alcoholics and dope fiends three times his age. Ned would carry the mark of this dishonor with him for the rest of his life – or as long as he lived in Oakland. It was possible that one day Ned would end up shooting Mike or Cobra to death. It was more likely that they would grow up and put an end to him. What happened that day would make them enemies for life. That's how it is in these streets. Respect means more than money.

Drama knelt down to console Ned. "You put up a helluva fight, champ. Except for that little snitching problem you got, you got nothing to be ashamed of.

Ned clenched his eyes together until the tears ran out. "I hate you, Drama," he muttered.

Drama giggled, "Yeah, well, remember once you told me that you was trying to decide whether you wanted to be a lawyer or a gangsta?

"Yeah…."

"Nigga, be a lawyer. You ain' built for this here."

Ned rubbed his eyes with the balls of his fists. He squinted and shook his head. "You cheated, Drama. You said I could have the fifty if I kept my mouth shut. Then you put Li'l Mike on me. When I started whuppin' Li'l Mike's ass you put Cobra on me. It was two against one. You ain' fair, Drama."

Drama gave a bitter laugh. "Well, I got three things to say to that. First, I gave you the fifty. It was up to you to hold on to it.

"Second, life is not fair, my nigga. Get used to that and learn.

"Number three, keep my name out your mouth 'cause next time I won't be nearly this friendly or polite. The chances are you won't even see it coming."

"I'm going to tell her, Drama. I'm going to tell Mamacide what you did," Ned cried out.

"Tell her what, snitch? I ain't lay a fingerprint on you," Drama said.

Drama spit on the sidewalk and then turned his back on Ned. "C'mon, y'all. Let's go. Firstborn wanted to talk to me about something."

Instinct made me reach for Ned. He held on to my hand, and I yanked him to his feet. When he let me go there was blood on my hand.

CHAPTER
THIRTEEN

THE PACIFIC WIND BLEW OUR BAND OF LOST SOULS DOWN THE desolation of International Boulevard. Virus skulked, shoulders drooped and head down, in Drama's footsteps. Every 30 seconds he'd turn around to view the world behind us. He never did this without tucking his hand beneath his black hoodie. That cannon on his waistband was our insurance policy.

Drama sipped from his Pepsi, occasionally making small talk. It was clear that his mind was somewhere else. He was probably thinking about money and how he could make more of it. I'm telling you that I knew this cat and how his mind is wired. We walked at both sides of him, clearly under the influence of his swagger.

A tall, lanky high school kid crossed from the opposite side of the street and started jogging toward us. He must have been from our hood, because when he drew close to us nobody flinched. His jog took him straight up to Drama.

"D," he said. "You heard what happened to Tall Frank, right?"

Drama stared through him and kept walking. A slight frown seemed to crease the corners of his lips. Undaunted, the teenager kept talking.

"That nigga was platinum, D."

Drama stopped walking, and so did we. A deep crease formed in Drama's forehead. His eyes narrowed. "You know who did it?" he asked the kid.

"I know the nigga. They call him Li'l Murda. I'm kinda cool with his brother, Steph. We shoot hoops together sometimes."

Drama started gagging on his Pepsi. He dropped the bottle as though it had lava inside. Glass fragments scattered everywhere. Petey slapped Drama's back as the hood god struggled to get his breath. Drama waved him off. His face turned a bright crimson.

The kid took a step backward, clearly shocked by Drama's sudden fit of rage. Drama took two steps toward him. They were almost nose to nose. Drama's voice rose to volume 10.

"You cool with Steph? Nigga, is you out your damn mind! They are our enemies. It's funk on sight. Every time you see that nigga, you s'posed to be on his helmet," Drama hollered.

The kid was trembling. Drama stabbed him in the chest with his forefinger. "Let me sprinkle some game on you, young homie. You cool with Steph? You should be looking to deal Steph off the face of planet Earth. You feel me, blood?" The circle around them drew tighter.

"Cool with Steph? You shooting hoops with a nigga when you should just be shooting. Blood, you should be plotting on how you gonna make them fools pay for what they did to our dead homie, and you busy socializing. I'll be damned...."

Ours was the most active hood in the city of death and cocaine. And this is how it got that way. Like so many before him, an older cat – Drama, in this case – was pushing this kid toward doing something he clearly did not want to do. And he was probably going to do it. Nobody wants to be labeled a sucker down here. It's not healthy. If you come from a war zone where survival is something you have to navigate every day and where respect from hustlers, gangstas, and killers is respect just the same, you want to be known as a real nigga, a bonafied nigga. You want people to point at you as you walk by and whisper, "That nigga is about what he says he's about."

Of course, the kid offered some weak excuses for not wanting to commit murder. Drama's response was, "It's murder only if they catch you."

"I could get life," the young man said.

"Juvenile life," Drama corrected. "Juvenile life ain' nuthin'."

Nuthin'. Nuthin' was at least 20 years. This was the world we came from. A planet where the family systems were broken, the schools had failed, the politicians had thrown up their hands, the preachers were hiding out behind the stained-glass windows, the jobs had fled, and the clocks spun backward.

Since I still had a voice with these cats, I thought it was time I broke in and used it. "Why don't you let young homie give Steph a pass this time, Drama?" I suggested.

War Thug sneered. Drama waved his hand, dismissing my idea out of hand. "A pass? The only pass he getting is an all-expense-paid-trip to hell…. Firstborn talking 'bout a pass."

Drama glanced back at the kid sideways and said, "Be about what you say you about."

The kid nodded at Drama like a subject bowing before a king. Drama turned his back and the kid half walked, half ran in the opposite direction. My heart sank as I watched the child soldier fall out of sight.

We had reached the Sugar Bowl grocery store by this time. I grabbed the door handle, but before I could enter, a gravelly voice startled me. It stopped me dead in my tracks.

"Godfather Firstborn."

The voice belonged to a chubby little man with an unkempt salt-and-pepper afro. He sat cross-legged on the sidewalk at the store's entrance. The gaping holes in his boot soles faced approaching patrons.

What a difference a day makes! Eddie G. was a hustling dynamo back years ago when crack had consumed much of Oakland. He had a fleet of luxury cars and a different fashion model on his arm every time I saw him. And then he got caught with that ki of raw in his trunk. He came out of prison seven years later and tried to jump back in the game. It didn't work. The game was moving twice as fast. The youngsters were three times more ruthless. By that time, Drama was waist deep in the streets. He wouldn't put Eddie G. on. Eventually, he was enslaved by the same product he once sold.

I was reaching in my pockets before he even called my name. I knew what was coming as soon as I saw Eddie's lips start moving. "Firstborn, I ain't seen you a minute black man. How you been? Remember back in the day when I used to give y'all money so you could take your little girlfriends to the movies? I used to say, 'Trick, they supposed to be paying your way in….'"

Before he could finish reciting my entire life history, I hit him off with five dollars. He gingerly plucked it out of his hand with his thumb and fingertips. Eddie G. looked up at me like I had just slammed him in the jaw with a set of brass knuckles. "Five dollars? That's all?"

Before I could answer, he looked over to my left and said, "Drama, I need to borrow some money."

Drama sucked his teeth as he reached into his pocket.

"How much?"

"Twenty."

Drama looked at me like Eddie G wasn't there and said, "You see, Firstborn, that's why I can't keep no money."

He reached into his pocket and pulled out a fat knot held together by a red rubber band. Drama licked his thumb and started flipping through the pile of money. There didn't seem to be anything in there smaller than a fifty. Eddie's eyes grew wide. "Man, I'll take one of those," he said pointing at a hundred. Drama snickered. He flipped his head toward the corner store and said, "C'mon, Firstborn. Come in this store with me. We'll break one of these bills and hit OG off with something."

My head was swimming from what I had seen. A little more than a year ago, we were on the corner selling loose joints. Now Black Christmas was flipping bricks. Drama had more shine in these streets than Jay-Z at the MTV awards.

As we approached the store, he moved to the side so I could open the door for him. It was one of those rare occasions when I would be able to speak to him alone. I decided to ask him something that had been racing around in my mind for 24 hours.

"How long can this last, Drama?"

His gold teeth flashed when he spoke. "I don't think a lot about tomorrow. It don't really go with what we trying to do out here. But you know that."

Drama took a careful glance at everyone in the store before he walked in. Satisfied there was no danger, he sauntered toward the counter. The man who owned the store knew a potential problem when he saw it. He stopped stocking his shelves and rushed over to Drama. He nodded with both hands out, open palms, as though he were preparing to surrender. Drama turned to me and said, "First, just promise me that you'll look after my mama after I'm gone. You want some snacks, a sandwich or something?"

"I don't want anything."

"Get something so I can break this hundred."

I reached for some onion rings, a pack of Hostess cupcakes, and a bottle of cherry soda. I lined them up on the counter.

Drama threw a hundred dollar bill on top of the cupcakes.

"No change," the man behind the counter blurted abruptly. He stared at Drama from beneath his bushy black eyebrows, like he was expecting a confrontation.

"Whaaaa? As much money as we spend in this joint every day?" Drama said, a storm brewing in his voice.

"No change!" the man shouted through clenched teeth. "You want change all the time, but you no buy nothing."

"I'm buying the damn cupcakes. What you mean, I ain't buyin' nuthin'?" Drama answered.

The storekeeper folded his arms over his chest and glared at us, his lips poked out in a pout.

Drama pointed at a little kid who stood there staring at the mounting conflict. He was nursing a bottle of milk, waiting for the inevitable to jump off. "Shorty, do me a favor," Drama said. "Go outside and tell my niggas to come in here for a minute."

The kid didn't hesitate. He turned on his pivot foot and made tracks.

"No change!" the shopkeeper shouted again like he thought we hadn't heard him the first two times.

I could smell homicide. You see, this is how things go bad in the hood. I pictured the kid relaying the message and the reaction that was taking place outside. The store owner was a fool. Why didn't he just accept the money and give us the change. Well, too late for that now, I thought. It didn't take 10 seconds for Virus, Petey, Grimy Greg, and War Thug to come storming through the door, guns drawn.

A gray-headed woman next to me dropped a loaf of Wonder Bread on the floor and quickly shuffled toward the door. Other patrons followed her. The man behind the counter stooped to reach for something near his feet. He was too late.

Virus already had the banger pointed straight at his dome. Grimy Greg aimed a .9mm at his chest. The man started shouting in Arabic.

I heard something that sounded like a brick fall to the floor in a back room. I envisioned the owner's family in the back loading up.

"There's somebody in back!" I hollered.

Petey raced toward the back room, his pistol in the air.

"Don't shoot!" a voice cried out from the darkness. A young man with a white apron around his neck came out with his hands up. He looked like a college student. He must have been hiding back there.

Drama lived for moments like this. (How do you think he got the name Drama?) "Why do you have to get so disrespectful? I came in here to buy something. What, my money ain't good?" he said to the storekeeper.

The owner's lips flipped and flapped. And then it sounded like he was trying to recite the alphabet backwards. I couldn't make out a thing he was trying to say. Petey stared at the owner liked a hungry wolf staring at a smothered steak.

"Break yo'self, fool!" he hollered.

Saliva started dripping from the owner's bottom lip. I'm not sure he understood what "break yo'self" meant.

"Strip!" Petey screamed. "You gonna come up out of everything! Don't make me have to say it again!"

The owner started taking off his apron. He nodded for the young man to do the same. Drama grinned as he tapped the hundred dollar bill on the counter.

"Now, Petey, we ain't going there right now," Drama said. "We come in here every day. It just wouldn't be right. I just want to buy these goodies here for Firstborn."

I knew good and well Drama wasn't even remotely thinking about what just wouldn't be right. He didn't let Petey rob the man because either he didn't want me in the middle of a 211 or because he wouldn't have been able to come back for his favorite sandwiches after he robbed the man who made them. I took a deep breath. I was glad. Petey backed away from the counter without a word. Still, he didn't put the gun away.

The man's hands shook as picked up the bill. He pressed the buttons on the cash register. When it popped open, he took out the proper change and dropped it in Drama's hands like the money was on fire.

"Here, here!" he said.

Drama snatched the bills but let the nickels and dimes bounce on the countertop. "Now, see? You can make a good decision when you try," he said to the owner before he turned his back and walked out.

The rest of the pack came out of the store, guns drawn like Old West bandits. Eddie G was seated right outside the store where we had left him. Drama flipped a twenty at him. Eddie didn't even say thank you.

When Drama put his next foot down on the pavement, a parade of little kids came running up to the car. "Drama! Drama!" they hollered.

"Aww damn!" he moaned, but he was smiling.

He was reaching his hand into his pocket before they could reach him. A chubby kid with an afro got there first. Drama stuck a twenty into his hand.

"Yo, Shorty. Take these young 'uns in the store and buy 'em what they want. Make sure everybody get what they want."

An ebony girl with pigtails ran up and squeezed Drama's waist. Drama's eyes sparkled. He knelt down and embraced her. She ran off and joined the other little ones heading into the store. I recognized her. Her dad was doing life in Avenal on a murder bid. Her mom was just another struggling black woman trying to do the best she could in the hood.

The homies were following at 20 feet away. Our soldiers were close enough to get active if something broke out but far enough away so as not to be a nuisance.

Drama and I met another familiar face before we could hit the corner. It belonged to Tuff Love. He was a hard hitter, a legendary Latino gang banger. The two crime figures embraced. As they say in the streets, "game recognize game." The gang shot-caller was pushing a baby carriage.

Tuff Love was deep into the gang life. He was dressed head to toe in the color of the gang he represented: sneakers, laces, belt, shirt, jacket, hat – all gang identifiers. The woman next to him was silent. She was pretty, but her face had hard lines, and she wore too much makeup. Her hair was combed back into a ponytail. She was draped in the same color Tuff Love wore, shoes to hair ribbon. The bundle in her arms was Tuff Love's infant. The blanket was made of the gang's color. Just the crown of the baby's skull was visible to the world. It was covered with a tiny beanie. Guess what color it was? The baby was covered in its destiny.

"What up, Tuffy Tuff?" Drama asked as he wrapped up Tuff Love in a bear hug. Drama nodded in my direction. You remember my brother, Firstborn, don't you?" Tuff Love shook my hand and then pounded his right fist against his heart.

"You heard what happened, right?" he said. His eyes were smoldering with anger.

"What?" Drama asked.

"Fools was bussin' at me and my girl last week. Cowards didn't have the heart to run up. They started blasting from across the street."

"What you do?"

"I ain't done nothin', homie. I'm on paperwork. I can't be walking around with no toaster. Plus, I was with my girl and my baby. We were just going to the store."

They had caught Tuff Love slipping. All it takes is that short walk for your enemies to catch you out here, and it can be over for you…and your family.

"Damn vampires," Drama said.

"I told my girl to run, and I jumped on top of the baby carriage."

"I'm glad they missed," Drama said.

"They didn't miss."

Tuff Love pointed at the front of the baby carriage. "Look man."

Drama and I bent over to examine the area where a baby's head would lay. Sure enough, there was a hole that went straight through. It was a bullet hole. I had seen enough of them to know.

Tuff Love said, "It's a miracle they didn't hit the baby."

"Who did it?" Drama asked.

"You know who it was," he said.

We all knew. The Guns, Cash, and Dope clique were Tuff Love's sworn enemies. They were ours, too, now that Drama had held them up for two or three kilos of raw. And that's not even mentioning the small fortune we had messed up on what they had fronted us. They probably hadn't meant to shoot at the baby. But the thing is, if you're with the situation then your family is too. Enemies won't always wait until you walk outside to shoot up your house. They'll bust slugs at your window, not knowing or caring who's inside. If someone is hunting you and they catch you slipping, anybody who's with you can get it. And sadly enough, if someone is shooting at you and your kids are with you…. Well, nobody who's real in these streets will tell you this can't happen.

"It's funk season, homie. You know we with you, right?" Drama declared.

The way I figured it, Latin Caesar and the killers he ran with should have blown up Drama within two days after the robbery. Now, I saw how Drama had stayed alive. Black Christmas Mob must have allied itself with Tuff Love's set, AHS (Almighty Hitters Squad). AHS was connected to a gang with a nationwide membership – Latin Caesar's sworn enemies. Someone once said, "The enemy of my enemy is my friend." The Black Christmas Mob had some new teammates. Drama was nothing if not resourceful.

Without a word of explanation, Tuff Love took the baby from its mother's grasp. He gently placed the infant in Drama's arms. Drama embraced the baby like a priest offering the child the rite of baptism. He kissed the baby's forehead and then handed it back to the mother.

"For the children," Drama said.

"For the children," Tuff Love echoed. He and his family made their way toward home. Drama and I stood watching them walk away.

A teardrop glistened in Drama's right eye. He looked at me and said, "Firstborn, nobody should be messing with no kids. Nobody."

It was then that I saw my chance. "Drama, that's just what I was saying about Crayon. She's just a child…a little girl. Homie, you have to help me get that young girl away from Phenomenal," I said.

He said nothing.

"I COULD APOLOGIZE FOR THE MEN WHO USED YOU AND MISUSED YOU, BUT IT WOULD NEVER BRING BACK WHAT THEY STOLE FROM YOU."

CHAPTER
FOURTEEN

AMBULANCE SIRENS WOKE ME THE NEXT MORNING. I WAS SUR-prised at how unaccustomed I had become to the sounds of the city after living in the wooded areas of a college campus. German shepherds barked as they strained at their leashes. Earth, Wind, and Fire sang "Shining Star" from the next door neighbor's stereo. Voices were coming from the living room. I went into the bathroom to wash up, and then I walked into the kitchen.

Crayon sat there at the kitchen table staring into a cup of cocoa. Light streaming in from the window made her look even younger than her years. Crayon twirled her hair with her fingers. She was so deep in thought she didn't hear me walk in.

"Are you really pregnant?" I asked.

"I think I might be," she said. Still looking down she said, "I'm sorry, Uncle Firstborn, about what Black Hole did. I hate him."

When I shook my head, the pain reminded me of the brute. I was lucky to still be alive; so was she. She sat there motionless, counting the spaces between my toes. Crayon rarely looked me straight in the eyes. I felt uncomfortable with that, and so I mentioned it.

"Crayon, why is it that you always look down when you speak to people. You don't like bald-headed black men or something?"

"Oh, no, Uncle Firstborn!" she said. "I just feel so ashamed of myself sometimes. I hurt inside. I think I'll never be right again."

There was one question that remained a mystery to me. I decided to ask it right then and there. "Crayon, how did you get hooked up with Phenomenal?"

"I was in that group home, Uncle Firstborn. I hated that place. I had never been in a situation like that. My mama was locked up. My daddy was locked up. Granny was in an institution. Auntie Maggie was dead. It was just me. I didn't have anybody to turn to. You don't know what it's like having to wake up every day in a room full of total strangers. Sometimes you come home from school and find out somebody's been all through your personal stuff. People stealing stuff like lipstick and tampons from under your mattress. Some of the girls want to fight you just because they're bored and they want somebody they can take out their frustrations on.

"I only had one friend – Betty. She slept in the bed next to mine. She didn't have any family. She was a white girl. She and I went to the same high school. She would always talk about her boyfriend. Everything was, 'My boyfriend this and my boyfriend that.' Then one day she said she had told her boyfriend about me and that he wanted to meet me. I said, 'Okay.' Anything to get out of that house for a few hours.

"He was a nice dude with a pretty car. He took us to get our nails done that first day. The next day, he took us to the movies. Pretty soon, my friend ran away from the house. I never saw Betty again, but the dude gave me a cell phone and kept calling me. We still went out.

One day, he told me he wanted me to come over to his house. He had this bad crib down by Lake Merritt. It had a fish tank with real sharks in it. We sat down on the couch drinking champagne. He told me he wanted me to be his woman. One thing led to another, and I ended up spending the night. The next morning, I told him I was going to get in trouble because I broke curfew. He told me that if I loved him, I didn't have to go home. I could just stay with him."

Crayon laughed. "Phenomenal told me that Betty had run away. He didn't know where she was. I knew Phenomenal had other girlfriends. I looked through his phone one day while he was asleep. There were a million girls' pictures on that phone. That was cool, long as I was his number one."

It was hard for me to believe she couldn't see the cold part coming. Like she said, she knew he had other women. She probably thought she was the one woman who could change him. I waited for her continue.

"Uncle Firstborn, you looking at me real sick right about now," Crayon said. "And I know what you're thinking. Let me help you. No bitch start out hoing. One day, after I been at the crib for two weeks, Phenomenal came home and said, 'Crayon, I'm in trouble. I don't know what I'ma do!'

"I asked him, 'Whassup?'

"He said, 'I need money to pay the rent. I put some money out on the street, and my man got popped by the narcs. Now I'm soaked. I don't know what I'ma do!' Now, Uncle Firstborn, this was a thoroughbred nigga talking. I had bet everything on him."

"He was playing you, sis. You couldn't see that?" I asked.

"I see it now, but then I was like…this is the only man I ever been with like that. This is my nigga. I'm going to do what I have to do to hold him down, feel me? If that meant hitting a lick, putting in some work, boosting...I was down.

"As it turned out, Phee had an idea about how we could come up. Phee had this uncle. He used be sitting around Phee mama house drinking Olde Gold. He always smelled like cat piss. His old ass used to be staring at my thighs with these big, bug eyes. I would shiver sometimes. He looked like the boogie man from a horror flick. I was scared of him. And then Phee said, 'Uncle Filbert say he'll break us off a big piece of money if you spend an hour with him.'"

Crayon's eyes spread wide as she relived her nightmare. "I told him, 'Phee, I'm not like that. You're the only man I've ever been with. I could never give myself to someone I didn't love.'

"Phee said, 'Love or money. It's all the same. You'll be doing this with him because you love me.'

"He started rubbing my back. He say, 'Crayon, I got two other bitches out on track humping their brains out, putting their lives on the line for me everyday. Now, I love you, baby. I ain' gonna be doing this forever. Once I get enough money, I'm going to buy me a house out in Modesto. I'm going to get married to the right woman. Now, I'm thinking you that right woman, but how can I marry a woman who won't take this all the way with me? These other chicks will sacrifice. How can I marry a woman who wouldn't sacrifice for me?'

"I started crying because I knew that the old me was 'bout to die. I felt like a caterpillar peeling off a layer of skin, except I was turning into a bug instead of a butterfly. I bowed my head and said, 'yes.'

"Fifteen minutes later, Uncle Filbert was at the crib. He brought the money. I had to go in the bedroom with him. He had a bad rash on his private parts, and he smelled like a stopped up toilet. It was like I had to split in two. I had to tell myself that I was somebody else. It was like I was standing outside of myself, watching myself do this ugly thing for the man I loved. Uncle Filbert was slobbering in my ear telling me how much he loved me. I was 14. He was like 60.

"When I finally came out of the room, Phee was sitting on the couch watching the game. He looked at me up and down like I was a Hefty bag full of dog poop. I was snotting and crying and the only thing he could say was, 'Take a shower and get dressed. We're going out.' His voice was different. He talked to me like I was a stranger.

"Phenomenal had told me he had two girls hoing for him. There were really eight. I met all of them that night. They lived in a tore-up hotel in the hood. They slept four to a room.

"Le Le, was his bottom broad. While Phee stood there watching and shaking his head, she broke down the rules of the game.

"I told Phenomenal, 'I ain't down with this. I ain' no ho. I want to go back to the group home.'"

I couldn't breathe. You could hear ants crawl on the pavement outside, it was so quiet in the apartment.

"And then what happened?" I asked.

"Phenomenal said, 'Bitch, you owe me money. I've been feeding you, putting clothes on your back, driving you 'round like I was your damn chauffeur. I figure all that comes to two racks. Girl, you got two thousand dollars in your purse?'"

A tear dropped from Crayon's eye.

"Well, Uncle Firstborn, I don't have to tell you that I ain' had no two thousand dollars. Phee said, 'If you can't get my money tonight, you're going to work.'"

"What did you do?" I asked.

"What else could I do? Phee pulled a girl's picture out of his pocket, and he passed it around the room. Some of them hos gasped when they looked down at it. Some cussed when they saw the photo. Everybody looked scared. You see, this girl had gone to the po po on Phenomenal. She was going to press charges. They had her in witness protection. They say she slipped away and came back to Oakland. I think it's true. In fact, I think she came back to warn me about Phenomenal. I acted like I didn't recognize her, but I did. You see, Uncle Firstborn, the girl in the picture was Betty. She was the chick who had introduced me to Phenomenal. She was never seen again after she came back to Oakland. That night, Phee took the picture back and then he pulled out a cigarette lighter and burned it."

Suddenly it dawned on me. She was trying to say that Phenomenal had killed this girl to stop her from testifying against him.

"A picture doesn't mean anything. He could have had that photo taken before she disappeared," I said.

"That's the thing, Uncle Firstborn. She was holding a newspaper up to her face in the picture. You could see the date on it. The picture was took the day after she disappeared. And that chick wasn't smiling. She looked scared as hell. Phee took that picture as a warning to the rest of us. I went out to the track with them that night. They told me what to do. It was disgusting. It was worse than dying. The next morning, I came back to the hotel with the other girls."

Crayon folded her hands in her lap. They were shaking.

"Aren't you tired?" I asked.

"Hell, yeah, I'm tired, but what else can I do? There's no out from the game. Phenomenal would kill me. Besides, I love him. Phee is a bonafide hustler. He a real nigga."

"Yeah, he's a real nigga all right," I said. "I hope you can say that after some diseased trick leaves you with fifty dollars and a good old-fashioned case of herpes simplex II. You protect yourself at least, don't you?" I asked.

"Most times, but some tricks like to hit it raw, and they pay extra. Phee say take the money; ain't nuthin' going to happen. He gives me birth controls," she said.

"Birth control pills don't stop HIV," I said, almost shouting. "Phee say it does."

Crayon dropped her head in her hands and began to weep inconsolably. "I'm so lost. I'm so lost. What I'ma do? What I'ma do?" she kept asking.

I was speechless. I couldn't understand. Being a man, how could I relate? I mean this little girl had been abandoned, pawed over, beaten up, and misused. But she was still somebody. I reached out and grabbed her hand.

"Let me tell you something, Crayon," I said. "After my grandmother died, I lived with a foster family for awhile. Mrs. Crenshaw had five or six of us squeezed up in her little house. She was a really sweet lady, for the most part. But she was funny about one thing – her good china. We ate on the good china only once a week; that was Sunday afternoon. Most of the time, we ate off the regular plates.

"All of the kids had to take turns washing and drying dishes. My turn to dry dishes came on Sunday afternoon. I'll never forget it because it was Super Bowl Sunday, and I was trying to hurry up so I could get finished and see the game. This kid handed me a soapy plate. I was trying to dry it with one eye on the plate and the other eye on the game in the next room. The one eye watching the plate let me down; I dropped Mrs. Crenshaw's good dinner plate.

"That white-haired woman came running into the other room screaming, 'Mama Gracie's good dinner plate! Mama Gracie's good dinner plate!'

"I said I was sorry, but she started crying and wouldn't stop. Mama Gracie's plate had come out to California from Louisiana and had been in the family since near the end of slavery. And I learned something that day. You can say, 'I'm sorry,' all you want, but some things you just can't replace.

"Crayon, in a way you're just like that dinner plate. I could apologize for the men who used you and misused you, but it would never bring back what they stole from you. What they broke was invaluable. It was like they looted the treasury of an ancient kingdom. They took stuff from you that nobody can replace.

"Mrs. Crenshaw shocked me, and she hurt me when she started crying. But after awhile she stopped and threw her arms around me. 'Boy, I forgive you,' she said. 'We just going to go on from here.' She pointed at the china closet. There were about 80 other plates in it just like the one I broke. Mrs. Crenshaw could pick herself up because there was still so much left.

"Crayon, they stole from you. They took that which no one can put back, but there is still so much left: so much pride, beauty, glory, and brilliance. You are a precious, precious black woman with so much to shower on this universe, so much to teach us all. You have so much love inside of you. Girl, you are a diamond. I'm not that religious, but I have picked up one thing from what I've read in the Bible. You are God's masterpiece, His undisputed perfection. Honey, you just have to hold your head up and keep on."

Crayon started crying. So did I.

CHAPTER
FIFTEEN

OLIVER DROPPED BY LATER THAT AFTERNOON. "COME ON, YOUNG blood," he said. "We're going to take a little ride."

I didn't ask where; I just followed him out the door. Minutes later, we were in his car speeding down the street. Oliver was silent. I could tell there were a million thoughts whizzing around inside of his skull, almost all of them having to do with me.

"What's up, O?" I asked.

He ignored me.

The car zoomed down International and then made a right on 82nd. We were headed to Uncle Al's house. Uncle Al practically raised Oliver. He was a former member of the Black Panther Party of Self Defense. He didn't wear the beret any more, but I'll bet if you woke him up in the middle of the night and asked him to recite the 10-point program, he could do it. It was said that Uncle Al slept with a Bible on one side of the bed and a rifle on the other, a holdover from his days in the Panthers.

I noticed that there were more cars parked in front of his house than usual. The curtains were spread open. As I followed Oliver up the concrete walkway, I stared at the faces in the picture window. A pretty, light-skinned woman with a dreadlock ponytail sat across from an older woman in a dashiki.

When I first met Oliver, he took me to a church service. The minister had once been a hard hitter in the streets, and I really thought he had something to say. He was sitting at the table wearing a Golden State Warriors jersey.

Uncle Al came to the door before Oliver could knock. He threw his arms around Oliver. That was the first time I had seen O smile that day. Oliver walked over the threshold. I followed and got the same bear hug from Uncle Al.

"Good morning, Firstborn. How are you, youngsta?"

"Cool," I said.

He smiled, examining the bruises on my face.

"Come in, y'all. Let's get right to it."

The whole place smelled like strawberry incense. Curtis Mayfield's anthem, "Future Shock," played in the background like a soft threat. A floor-to-ceiling portrait of Huey P. Newton's head covered most of the living room wall. It had been painted in light blue and black tones.

Two empty chairs remained at the kitchen table: one for Oliver and one for me. I took the seat across from Oliver.

Uncle Al cleared his throat.

"Now, I don't know if everybody here knows everybody." He went on to make the introductions.

The pretty woman with the long dreads was Wilona Washington. She was a women's rights activist here in the Bay. She looked to be about 25.

Debra Thursday sat across from her. Debra headed a chain of safe houses for teenage girls seeking to escape prostitution.

Finally, there was the good reverend. He introduced himself as "Reverend Ray." His full name was Reverend Raymond Fuller. He had a broad smile and a firm handshake.

"I remember you, Reverend," I said.

"I remember you, Firstborn," he countered. That surprised me because I'm sure he had shaken thousands of hands since the last time he'd seen me. We really hadn't even spoken. He gave me a prophesy. He said that if I was playing around in a dark world and didn't get out, something bad was going to happen to someone who was close to me. When my girlfriend Maggie was stabbed to death, I remembered his words.

"I hear you're back in the Town to do some good," said Reverend Ray.

I cleared my throat. "Depends how you look at it."

He raised an eyebrow. "How's that?"

I answered, "Ms. Holmes, the church lady I'm staying with, says that 'Sometimes people in the ghetto have to do some evil to get some good out of life.'"

The reverend sat back in his chair like I'd just said the most ridiculous thing he'd ever heard. "'Whatsoever a man soweth, he shall also reap.' That's what the Bible says. If you throw evil seeds in the ground, you are going to get back evil. Be careful, son. Not everyone who goes to church is a student of the Bible."

Oliver growled under his breath, "Ms. Holmes is so full of..."

"Oliver! There are ladies present!" Uncle Al was from the old school. He really didn't play that cussing-in-front-of-women thing.

Wilona Washington jumped into the conversation. "Firstborn, Oliver ain't no snitch. He didn't go into the whole story, but we do know you're trying to get a young woman off the corner. I think that's admirable."

Oliver slammed his hand down on the kitchen table. Everyone jumped. "It's the type of admirable thing that can get a nigga kilt."

Reverend Ray spoke again. "Firstborn, I think you have to look beyond this little girl. I mean, maybe God has opened your eyes to this problem because you're supposed to help free a whole generation. These young people need to hear from somebody who has walked in their shoes, somebody from their world. They need someone who can speak their language. Dr. King was only 26 years old when the Montgomery bus boycott jumped off. The saying is old people for counsel; young people for war. Maybe God has bought you back here to be a warrior for justice and righteousness."

There was a thought that had never entered my mind. Now, it entered and kept on traveling, but before I could dismiss it entirely, Oliver said, "I have a lot of respect for the rev here, Firstborn. You might want to pay some mind to what he's saying."

I wasn't religious, but I had been brought up to respect religious people, especially people like the reverend, because he was for real. But I was going to have my say.

"Reverend Ray," I said, "every block in the hood has three things: a liquor store, a church, and a funeral parlor. Now, I know why the liquor store exists. That's obvious; people are going to want to drown their pain. I know why the funeral parlor exists; sooner or later, we're all going to need it. But would you tell me why the church exists? I mean, in some places they're next door to each other or across the street from one another. You have hookers and hoodlums congregating 10 feet away from the church door, and in most cases, the church doesn't do anything to reach them. It's not like it was during the civil rights movement. Most churches have nothing to offer the hood but speeches and songs. These churches are disconnected from the hood. They don't speak our language. The church folks don't walk our streets. Most of the pastors are old enough to be my grandfather. They don't understand your average kid in the hood."

Every eye cut in Reverend Ray's direction. He took a sip of tea and smiled. He didn't seem moved at all. "You're right – at least partially – Firstborn. It's like this. Back during segregation all blacks lived in the same neighborhood. You had Mr. Johnson, the owner of the store living next door to Dr. Jones, the pediatrician. A kid with no father had role models to look up to. All of these churches you see were once supported and attended by people who lived in the community. Back when I was little, black people owned all the stores in the neighborhood.

"The blessing of the movement was that it opened doors that let us live out in the suburbs. And when that door opened, a great deal of the blacks with education and wealth walked through it. The middle class left the hood for the hills and the suburbs. We have our children in tap and ballet classes. We live on streets with palm trees, and we have swimming pools in our backyards. The problem is that not everybody got a chance to move out to Livermore or Walnut Creek. When the educated and successful blacks left for the suburbs, they left a vacuum behind them. The neighborhood became a hood. It happened all over the country, not just in Oakland. And so we come back in from the suburbs to go to church, but we don't have that day-to-day interaction with the folks who live in the hood. We don't share their reality."

"It's more about class than race," I said.

"In some respects, yes," Reverend Ray replied. "Sometimes, it's not that the people who come to our churches don't care. It might be that they look at the horrors that you and I grew up seeing, but they don't realize what they're looking at."

"...because, like you said, it's not part of their everyday reality," I said, finishing the thought.

"Right," Reverend Ray agreed.

Uncle Al chimed in. "How did we get here, y'all? In my day we talked 'bout 'power to the people.' Now I hear these young boys standing around on the corner talkin' 'bout how 'pimpin' and 'hoin' is the best thing goin'. Back in my day, we sat around and thought 'bout how we could stop police brutality in the ghetto and how we could get more of our people on the voter's roll. Now, these young kids are living in a state of suspended animation. They thinking they got it goin' on, but they ain't goin' nowhere but prison and the graveyard. The game is an illusion.

"The black community in Oakland is in a state of crisis. Every time a devastating reminder of that hits, they wheel out one of these so-called community leaders to speak for us. Half of these Negroes don't even live in Oakland. They just drive down here to make a speech and then flee to the safety of the suburbs before nightfall. Who speaks for us now? Which one of these so-called black leaders has the ear of those gangs, teams, and mobs?"

Ms. Thursday asked, "How high is the black race going to rise when y'all are calling women 'bitches' and 'hos' and telling young sisters they don't really love you if you they won't sell their bodies for you? Don't give me that 'How did we get here?' speech. Every time one of you men impregnated one of your sisters and walked away from her, every time you laughed at a joke about one of your sisters, or every time you said nothing when your brother called her 'bitch,' you brought us another step closer to the brink of annihilation."

Debra Thursday, shook her head. "Black women are strong. Harriet Tubman might have been the one who got in the history book, but we all have some Harriet in us. Firstborn, you tell this young girl, whoever she is, that she has the power to free herself. Tell her to believe in herself. Tell her that her higher power has destined her for a life of purpose and victory. Tell her to wait for her opportunity and make her break. There are those of us out here who will lay down our lives to help her make it to safety.

Debra handed me a brochure. Reverend Ray gave me his hand. "Firstborn, I'm about what I say I'm about. If you ever find out that I can help you in any way, just reach out to me. My church is looking for a way to get in this war. We're ready to get down. We can't just sit by and sing hymns while our little girls are being turned into whores right in front of the church door. We're ready to get out in these streets with the message of the Gospel."

Something in the reverend's eyes told me that he was for real. He pastored a church of almost a thousand members. If anyone could make a difference, he could.

Uncle Al snorted, "Firstborn, you know how I get down. I'm with you till the wheels come off, my young brother. If you need me, just call, and I'll be there with that little toy I keep upstairs by the bedside."

Oliver hit his forehead with the heel his hand. "Uncle Al, that's just what we don't need."

Uncle Al smiled, "Sure it is. Ain't you never heard that saying, 'Nothing stops a bullet like a nigga's hard head?'"

"No, no, no," Reverend Ray said. "The saying goes, 'Nothing stops a bullet like a job.'"

"Yeah, I knew it was something like that," Uncle Al said as he winked at me.

"EVERYTHING IS MONEY, MONEY, MONEY. WHAT IS GOING TO HAPPEN WHEN I CAN'T CASH HIM OUT ANYMORE?"

CHAPTER
SIXTEEN

THE NEXT DAY THERE WAS A KNOCK AT THE DOOR AROUND BREAK-fast time. I gathered my thoughts and emotions as Crayon came in the door and embraced Ms. Holmes. Crayon was beginning to look old around the eyes, I thought, as she smiled in my direction. I beckoned for her to have a seat at the table and pulled out a chair next to me. Ms. Holmes made oatmeal with raisins for us. I asked for some tea. It was mine in a microwave minute. Crayon set the hourglass on the kitchen table.

"Well, Crayon how does it all end?" I asked. I took a sip from my lemon rose tea and waited for her answer.

Her lips parted slightly as she stared down into her plate. I could see tears forming at the corners of her eyes.

"The end is death or Las Vegas." I could barely hear her words.

Death, I could understand. But Las Vegas? What did she mean?

"Sometimes I think Phee love me. He say he do. And other times, I'm just an ATM with breasts and high heels. Everything is money, money, money. What is going to happen when I can't cash him out anymore?"

She had a point. I had heard stories about the girls who could no longer earn. They were tortured with curling irons, set on fire, gang raped, and worse. Crayon told me three or four stories of young girls who had met grisly ends – teenage prostitutes who would never see the age of 21. And then it was like she ran out of breath. I looked down at her hands. Her fingertips were trembling.

Ms. Holmes broke the silence that had come by humming, "Precious Lord."

"What are we going to do, Firstborn?" Crayon asked.

I didn't know. My whole planet was falling off its orbit. I had walked and rode past young girls in Crayon's situation my entire life. I had accepted their plight the same way I accepted the fact that the Earth circles around the sun. It had become such a part of the landscape of the ghetto that I never questioned it.

Crayon jumped back into her stories of street life and death. As I heard story after story from Crayon's lips, I was beginning to see this tremendous tragedy in a brand new light.

I sat mesmerized as she told tales of 12-year-old girls snatched off the streets of Oakland by gorilla pimps and forced to be prostitutes. She told of a father who told his daughter, "You out here all the time anyway. You might as well make me some money." I heard the story of a girl who pimped her younger sisters on the track.

"But what about Las Vegas?" I asked.

Crayon leaned over the table, whispering in hopes that her grandmother might be spared what she was about to say. "I heard they have a house down there. It's one of those places where you might have to do 20 or 30 dates a day. You just wear out. Get sick. They got an iron door in the front and bars on the windows. Somebody watching you all the time. Once they get you inside, you can't get out."

Crayon stopped talking, so I took the discussion in a different direction. "That day when I came out there to get you, why didn't you say anything? I'll even go further than that. Why did you let that leech beat up your own grandmother?"

"I'm scared of Phenomenal, but I love him at the same time."

She stared into my eyes and then said with a sad smile, "You can't understand that can you?"

Surely, I could not.

"Sapphire's gone, I think to Las Vegas. Nobody wants to talk about it. When I came back from here yesterday they had my suitcase packed. I got this feeling I'm going somewhere. I think it's out of town. I think maybe I'm going to Las Vegas. If I never see you again, thank you, Uncle Firstborn. Look after Grandma. I'm so sorry."

She patted my hand. "Tell her that after I'm gone." She scrambled to her feet and raced out the door.

"Hold up girl!" I cried after her. But it was too late. The sand had dripped to the bottom of the hourglass.

"I WAS A LITTLE GIRL WITH EVERYTHING GOING FOR ME WHEN THEY PUT ME OUT ON THE TRACK. SOULLESS BASTARDS LIKE PHENOMENAL DESERVE TO GET HIT."

CHAPTER
SEVENTEEN

Gangstas live moment to moment. They don't do much planning ahead because you never know. That's why I wasn't surprised to get word that Drama was throwing a "welcome home" party for me late that afternoon. He had moved from the crowded, rundown second floor digs that he and his family had called home for years. His family rented a three-bedroom house a few blocks from where we'd grown up. Things were better.

Bass as loud as thunder struck me two blocks away from Drama's house. Bodyguards were posted at each end of the block. Grimy Greg and Virus threw up the Black Christmas Mob hand sign when I hit the corner. They scanned every car that turned onto the street. "Sleep is the cousin of death," was the Black Christmas Mob credo. That phrase was in full effect.

A '68 Ford Mustang slowed when it drew close. The windows were tinted so dark that I couldn't see who was inside, but I had no trouble understanding the voice that hollered out at me as the car glided by. "Welcome home, Firstborn!" It shouted. I flashed the peace sign.

Twenty feet away from the address on the paper, I heard Sideshow Psycho chatting Bay Area slang over hip-hop beats. Guests were heading through a narrow passage on the side of a cream-colored house. Two young brothers I didn't recognize blocked the entrance. Big smiles greeted me. A kid with corn rows and a long white tee wrapped me up in his arms. "Welcome home, Firstborn." I didn't know him from Adam.

The corridor opened up to a large backyard behind the house. This is where the party was jumping off. The twin aromas of malt liquor and marijuana marinated together. The d.j. threw on the old school Funkadelic "One Nation Under A Groove." It was then I saw him. He wasn't wearing a shirt. His jeans were sagging. He was wearing another pair of brand new Jordans.

When Drama turned around, I could see the words, "East Oakland," in a semicircle tattoo on his back. Drama, surrounded by three very pretty girls, was dancing in a circle. His braids jumped up and down as he bobbed his head and threw the Black Christmas hand sign in the air. A lit blunt was hanging out of his mouth.

Some of the older people were dancing right alongside Drama. They were neighbors and relatives, and they toasted the occasion with bottles of Miller Beer.

When Drama saw me he came out of the circle and grabbed me by the wrist. Before I knew it, I had been pulled me into the circle. Next came the war chant. This was the Black Christmas Mob theme song. Crewmembers twisted the song's hook. Like a thug choir they chanted, "Black Christmas under a groove!"

A fourth girl joined the circle. She grabbed my hands and started dancing with me. I'm not much of a dancer. And I'm pretty self-conscious. She didn't seem to mind. She was winking at me.

When the song ended, I hugged Drama's neck and asked, "Where's Ms. Velvet?" He pointed at two glass doors at the rear of the house. Ms. Velvet was Drama's mother. I called her my second mother. A smile spread across my face as I looked forward to seeing her again. Ms. Velvet was a Christian woman. She had nothing to do with this lifestyle. She had encouraged me to leave it alone before I left Oakland.

I slid the glass doors open and stepped down on the plush black carpet. There she was, sitting at a table, her transistor radio turned to the gospel radio station. Ms. Velvet was blind. She couldn't see me when I entered, yet she hollered, "Firstborn!" when I drew close.

"Ms. Velvet, how did you know it was me?" I asked. After all, I had not been back to East Oakland in a year.

She stretched out her arms for a hug. She smelled like baby powder. She wrapped me up in her big, meaty arms and rocked me back and forth. She patted my back three times. "I heard your footsteps," she said as she released me.

Ms. Holmes hated the devil's music. She hated his people. She hated his parties. But she had no problem with his barbecue. There was a big plate of spare ribs piled 13 inches high in front of her. As I took a seat next to her, she hollered into another room, "Sandra! Sandra!"

I held my breath. I hadn't seen Sandra since last summer's blood storm sent her boyfriend, Pimpin' Easy, down in a hail of bullets. I half stood as she entered the room. Sandra was about 10 years older than me, but I had grown up with a crush on her. She was fine, like one of those chicks in a hip-hop video. Or I should say, she used to be. Her hair was poorly combed, she had put on a good 30 pounds, and her shirt was hanging out of her pants. She looked like hell.

"What, you want mama?" she said, looking right at me.

"Baby, you the one with the eyesight. Don't you see Firstborn right there?"

"Yeah, so?"

There was a time that Sandra would have scooped me up in her arms and plastered kisses all over my face. She used to call me "Little Brother." I had a good idea why she was being so frosty. She thought I had something to do with the shooting death of her boyfriend, Pimpin' Easy. True, I saw it. I even knew who did it, but I didn't know what was going down until the bullets started banging out.

"It wasn't me, Sandra," I said. "I didn't know anything about it until it happened."

Sandra rolled her eyes but said nothing.

"Didn't know what, Firstborn?" Ms. Velvet asked.

"Sandra knows what I mean, Ms. Velvet."

Just then, the glass doors slid open and Drama walked in. He had a fresh blunt dangling between his lips. He toted a bottle of Moet by the neck. "Firstborn, come on outside. Dey some fine bitches out here, wanna holla at you, playa!"

"Drama, watch your mouth. Don't you see your mother sitting here!" I said.

"Oh, 'scuse me, Ma. What I meant to say was, there are some upstanding young members of the female species who wish to become acquainted with Firstborn."

Sandra laughed. Ms. Velvet shook her head. "Boy, did I hear crap shooting and gambling on the side of my house a little while ago?" she asked.

"You sure did, Mama. Ain't you always tell me that the Bible say, 'Man should work by the sweat of his brow?' Well, these niggas is out here sweating me today. They got a good five hun'ed out my pockets before I walked away to get them ribs going."

Drama threw one his arms across my shoulders. "Come on burn one of these trees with a playa, now."

As Drama led me outside to the barbecue smoke and sunlight, his mother hollered at my back. "Firstborn, life is too brief to wander around in the darkness. Don't get led astray." I turned around to wave, but then I remembered that she couldn't see.

Petey and Mamacide slapped dominoes down on a folding table. OGs sat around telling old hood stories. "Hi, D!" a thick-built girl with a redbone complexion hollered. A smile stretched across Drama's face. He looked down at a little boy I guessed to be five. The pretty redbone female was toting him by the arm.

"Come here, little man!" Drama hollered. The kid took off running for Drama's outstretched arms. Drama scooped him up in his arms and lifted him high in the air. "This is my stepson, Firstborn!" he announced. The mother beamed. Drama gave a squeeze and then put the young kid down.

"Tell Aunt Sandra to fix you something to eat, Michael." Drama ordered, patting the kid on the back. He took off with his mother in tow.

After they were out of earshot, I said, "Stepson?"

"Yeah!" Drama snickered. "I'm stepping over him to get to his mama."

I couldn't help but laugh. I know it was foul, but he caught me off guard with that one. And you have to admit it was funny. "Drama you ain't even right," I said between giggles.

After I had composed myself, we walked in the direction of a cocoa-complexioned girl leaning against a fence. Dimples creased her cheeks when she smiled. She stood up against the fence with a glass of chilled wine in her hand. "Firstborn, this is Diane," Drama said. "She's a first-year social work major at Berkeley. She wants to come back here and save the world when she graduates." He didn't crack a smile. He meant what he had just said.

Drama put his hand on my shoulder and pointed at me like he was selling laundry detergent on a TV commercial. "Firstborn here is studying journalism at San Jose State University. You all have a lot in common. He's also one of your save-the-world types. Take it easy on him. He's my brother."

I reached out my hand for Diane's hand.

"Well," Diane said, "I know for a fact that Drama doesn't have any real brothers, just a sister. For him to call you that is quite something. You two must be very close."

"Yes," I said. The thing was, I didn't want to talk about me. I wanted to find out all about the beautiful woman behind those gorgeous brown eyes.

"What are you doing here?" I asked. It was an honest question. Her English was perfect. She seemed cultured and refined. She stood out from the sea of hoochie mamas and hood rats that Drama had invited to this get-together. As it turned out, she was a student of literature. We got into a great discussion of James Baldwin's later works. She fascinated me, so much so that I felt a sense of anger when Sandra called me. She called me twice and then summoned me with a flip of her hand.

"Diane, can I have your phone number?" I asked. She nodded and smiled. I thanked her for the conversation, and then I followed Sandra to the front of the house.

Sandra's mood had changed. She kissed my cheek. "I believe you," she said.

We sat down on the steps. More people were walking up to the house. It would soon be night, and the music was still at volume 10. I felt sorry for the neighbors.

We took a seat on the front steps. "What's up?" I asked.

"I'm tore up, Firstborn."

I didn't know what to say.

"Pimpin' Easy was my whole life. I loved him."

"Sandra, it wasn't much of a life. I mean God bless the dead. Rest in peace and all that. But let's keep it real. That fool was a bottom-feeding pimp. I almost want to say that the world is better off with him dead."

She raised her voice, "Firstborn, that's my husband you're talking about!"

"Sandra save that for some square who doesn't know any better. This is me you're talking to."

"I remember last year you were that square."

I shrugged. "Things change. So enough about me. What about you, beloved? What are you doing for yourself? You've already lost the race if your life is so wrapped up in some Negro that you can't find the way to the ladies' room without him giving you directions. I know you're stronger than that, Sandra."

"Yeah, it's just that everybody wants somebody in their life."

"Baby, you have to learn how to enjoy your own company. Pamper yourself. Spoil yourself. Get in the business of making Sandra's dreams come true. Go to college. Treat yourself like a queen. And if a dude says that he wants to be down, but he can't sign on to treating you like the very special woman are, tell him to kick rocks. For the first time in your life, it's got to be all about Sandra."

She reached over and kissed me on top of my head. "I love you little brother," she said. "You know I always say that God made a mistake. You should have been my brother instead of Drama."

"I am your brother," I said.

"You damn right," she agreed. "And I know why you came back. I was a little girl with everything going for me when they put me out on the track. Soulless bastards like Phenomenal deserve to get hit. Do you know he keeps those poor slave girls in a hotel room with no windows while he lives like an oil sheik?"

I raised my eyebrow but said nothing.

"Y'all need to scrape Phenomenal. Clap some steel on a fool. Serve that nigga! Have I made that clear?"

"Perfectly," I said. Now, if only I could persuade Drama.

CHAPTER
EIGHTEEN

"COME ON LET'S GO FOR A WALK, BRUH," DRAMA SAID.

I hugged Sandra's neck and then followed Drama down the walkway and to the sidewalk. We walked for two blocks and then perched on someone's stoop. It was almost dark.

Our neighborhood was deceptive. Nothing was actually what it appeared to be. For instance, that night Drama looked like any other working dude sitting next to a good friend discussing the results of the game. He was talking about the game all right – the dope game, not the baseball game. Drama was running the most lucrative business in the entire community from that stoop. From that vantage point, he could see almost everything.

As long as you have poor people in America with restricted opportunities, you will have the drug game. The global economy has sent millions of jobs and billions of dollars overseas. It has also birthed a kill or be killed culture in ghettoes like this, where street knowledge might seem of more value than book knowledge. With no education and no viable job skills, young people are drawn into the quagmire of quick loot and near certain death or incarceration. Add to that stew the glamorization of the game by hip-hop culture and you have the recipe for genocide. I had watched too many of my peers slide into the abyss. You wonder how drug deals could take place with constant police patrols all around?

Sure, the police were watching us, but we were watching them watch us. Drama had senior citizens who needed a boost to their social security checks staring out of second story windows with binoculars. Young kids who couldn't get a paper route worked on the ghetto bread grind. They stood perched on rooftops and street corners, timing police patrols and scouting out undercover cops.

I heard a series of sharp whistles and birdcalls all around me. Two minutes later, a black-and-white slowed. My heart jumped into my throat, but Drama hardly flinched. He scanned from one end of the block to the other, but his head never moved. The police car stopped just a few feet in front of us. I was calculating whether we could pop up from the stoop and outrun them. Drama sat up. He didn't recognize the numbers on top of the squad car. He peered into the car searching to see who was inside.

The car door opened. Drama shook his head and cussed. The cop saw this and grinned.

"Don't even think about running!" she said.

It was the Hawk. Even though it was near dark, she wore her sunglasses. She marched toward us with her billy club in hand. She rolled her neck around her shoulders like she was flexing for a fight. In the game, she was the enemy. She had sent more brothers to the penitentiary than I could count. If you ever slipped out here, she was on you, and it was over. The working people loved her. If you really got off the chain, they were going to call her on you. If you were out here scrambling for diaper money or the monthly rent, you could become damage collateral in the path of her destruction.

"Firstborn, how you doing, black man? I ain't seen you in a minute!" she called as she approached me.

"I'm fine. I'm okay," I forced myself to reply.

"Where you been, young man?"

"College. I've been in college," I said.

The Hawk smiled. "I'm glad to hear that. Now, what you doing back here sitting next to Satan?"

Drama frowned. "When you going to stop harassing us, Hawk?" he asked.

"Nigga, I'm not harassing you. When I start harassing you, I'll be applying this billy stick to the tender part of your ass. Right now, I'm just a law enforcement officer conversing with the friend of a suspected drug kingpin. I hate you, Drama. And if it's the last thing I do before I retire from this job, I'm going to drag you out of this neighborhood in handcuffs. You're going to slip one day, and I'll be right there to step on your tail."

The Hawk smiled. It wasn't a real smile. It was the expression that said, "You have caught my full attention and your freedom is now hanging in the balance."

"Firstborn," she said, "it looks like God above done smiled on you. Don't throw away your blessings. Don't let me find you out here tomorrow. You're not built for this game. I don't want to take you down to Glen Dyer jail, baby. I've cut you some breaks because of who your daddy was to us, but you out of favors, son. Don't throw away your life. Go back to wherever it was you were."

The Hawk banged her billy club on the step where I was sitting. She turned and left without another word. I watched her ease into the passenger seat of the squad car. The driver punched the gas and the police car sped off in a cloud of asphalt pebbles and exhaust fumes. I took a deep breath and sighed my relief.

As soon as the patrol car drove off, Craig walked up to us. "What's up, D? How you been, Firstborn?" We both nodded. We had grown up with Craig. He was thinner now. He wore a T-shirt with Tupac's black and white image on it. It hung off him. He pulled his pants up. They were two sizes too big for him.

"How long you been home, playa?" Drama asked Craig.

"About two weeks."

"What you need, man?"

"A job."

"I don't know if you want to get down like that, potna. Ain't you on parole."

Craig's eyes belonged to an old man. He tucked both his fists in the pockets of his oversized pants. "Truth is, I can't get a real job. It's a million niggas with no prison record out here can't find a job. I can't make no money recycling cans. My little girl looking up at me like, "Daddy, I want ice cream. Daddy, I want to go to the movies.""

I stood up from the step so I could look Craig right in his eyes. "Look, brother man, it's not worth it. You hang in there. You'll find work. You get caught with a dub and your daughter won't have you in her life for a long time. She needs the presence of a father in her life more than she needs the material things. Who'll protect her from the pimps and the predators while you're gone?"

Craig gave me a sad smile. He put his hands behind his back and shifted from one foot to the other. "Firstborn, she's materialistic just like her mother. I hear what you're saying, and I appreciate that, bruh, really I do. The thing is, I can't eat that. My little girl's feet grow every day, and she ain't trying to see no Payless."

Drama pulled a pack of Kool cigarettes out of his pocket. He stuck one in his mouth and lit it. He took a deep pull and then exhaled. It smelled like hell smoke. "Playa, find War Thug and tell him I said to put you on," he said.

Craig shook our hands and then started down the block. Drama looked at me and laughed. He was a realist living in the Great Recession; I was an idealist living on planet Mars as far as he was concerned.

Tell me more about college, Firstborn," Drama said.

There was so much to say that I didn't know where to begin. "Well, in college, I've learned about all these incredible places. I'm saving up to go to Rome next summer. It's a school trip. I've never been anywhere, D. You know that? There's so much I want to see and do. When I graduate I want to go to Paris and write a book. Can you believe that?"

Drama smiled. "You can do it man. You can be anything you want to be. You just got to stay away from these streets, my brother. Jail is the last place you want to go, man. Once they get you on paperwork, you're screwed, dude. They own you. They got a license to harass you. Stay away from here. I'll help you get to Rome."

A '65 Mustang whizzed past. The driver beeped. Drama waved.

"Was that Knock Out?" I asked, recalling a friend we used to play basketball with.

"No. That wasn't no Knock Out! And don't ever mention that name in my presence again," Drama said.

Angry red waves formed across his forehead.

I was surprised. I kept silent.

"Knock Out turned snitch. I saw his name myself on the paperwork," Drama finally said with a sigh. "It hurt me to my heart. I mean, I don't understand these cats. You sell dope. You take your chances. One day the damn FBI kicks in your door with a warrant in hand. They get you in a room and tell you that you ain't never going home. They say they got you on video. They say there's collaborating testimony. They say basically, 'Nigga, you washed.' And then they tell you, 'Don't you want to help yourself? You give us some names and you can go home, or you can do 25 to life.' You start turning it over in your mind, and the next thing you know, you giving up cats you went to kindergarten with.

"How you going to marinate in the game if you afraid to go to jail? They call it the game for a reason, Firstborn! Sometimes you win, but the reality is that it could all end in the next two seconds. You will lose. It's only a question of when. You can never get that out of your mind. Truth is, I never seen nobody walk away from this and go lay out on the beach in Palm Springs for the rest of they life sipping Moet. One day you go to court and you don't come back, or you pull up to a red light and your enemies start feeding you hot lead. That's the nature of this game. The odds are seriously stacked against you. Why get in this if you can't face the consequences?"

Looney Larry, one of the Black Christmas Mob foot soldiers, approached us. He went up to Drama and whispered something in his ear. Drama nodded and said, "Yeah, give him a brick. He good for it. Tell him he got 10 days to come back with our money. Tell him I will show up at a nigga's mama house looking for him if my paper ain't right. And I'ma have my hyenas wit me. Make sure you tell him that, too."

I let Larry get a few feet away before I said anything else. "Drama, how long before one of these young guns out here decides to bang you out because they want to be the king?"

Drama sucked his teeth. "All this money would collapse tomorrow. Ain' one of these clowns smart enough to play my position. You see all of these cats smiling around here. That's because everybody eating. It's dangerous to mess with the man who putting food on the plate."

Drama was doing too much I thought to myself. The minute you lose your sense of paranoia in the dope game, you are doomed. Drama wasn't hungry anymore. I remember thinking, he's going to fall. In the hip-hop game, people stay alive album after album because they're hungry. And then something happens. Good living and success take away that hunger. Then their albums stop hitting. It's not that they're lazy or conceited. It's just that hunger is a motivator that cannot be duplicated or turned on or off like a switch.

The streets, in this case, function just like the hip-hop game. And Drama's hunger was gone. It was like he was in a sword fight without a shield. Sooner or later he was going to get struck down. I wondered if there was enough war left in him to handle someone like Phenomenal.

The moon fell down over Oakland. We watched the stars twinkle in the sky. For a long time we sat there, wallowing in our own private thoughts.

Ill Syl came pimp hopping up the steps, the soles of his shoes flapping loose. His cheeks were drawn together; he was stretched out tightly. He stood in front of us with his knees squeezed together and started rubbing his bare arms. He was trembling.

Ill Syl was suffering from chemical leprosy.

"I'm sick, Drama," he announced.

"Go see a doctor," Drama said matter-of-factly."

"Don't play with me, Drama. I'm dope sick. I need my medicine. I'm shaking."

"You got money?"

"I'm broke."

"Well, if you ain't got no money, you just gonna have to shake."

"But after all the money I spent with you and the Mob…"

Drama put the flat of his palm on his mouth and suppressed an exaggerated yawn.

"Syl, get ghost, man. Me and my nigga here is conversatin'."

Ill Syl shot Drama an evil glare. Drama was unmoved. He shooed him away like he was waving off a pesky fly. "These broke ass, niggas..." (Drama muttered like Syl wasn't even there) "...they always want something for nuthin'." Ill Syl walked away quickly, talking to himself. "And take a shower!" Drama hollered after him.

Drama was laughing, but I wasn't. Syl was a human being. No one should be disrespected like that, especially someone who has supported your lifestyle by placing thousands of dollars in your pockets. It was my turn to sprinkle some reality on Drama's life.

"Drama," I said, "Oakland is the fifth most dangerous city in the entire country. And you control the most dangerous five blocks in the most violent part of Oakland. You control the monster named Black Christmas. What does that make you?"

Drama's eyelids fluttered. "What does it make me? What does it make you? Has all of that book reading in college corrupted your memory? You and me created this beast together, remember? In fact, if my memory serves me right, you were the one who named it the Black Christmas Mob. So, nigga, you can't judge me. Your hands is just as bloody as mine."

What could I say to that? He was right. But if in the beginning I had any idea that we were creating this monster, would I have stayed on the train as long as I did? I'd like to think not. The problem is that none of us can ever really see the complete consequences of our actions and what the result of our decisions might be.

"Drama, is there anything you've done that you're ashamed of?" I asked.

Drama blew a blast of cigarette smoke at the stars. He cut his eyes in my direction. "I'm going to tell you something, but you have promise to keep this to yourself," he said.

"Have you ever told me something and heard it again somewhere else?"

Of course, he hadn't. He smiled slowly and said, "My sister. You were there. You remember when that fool Pimpin' Easy started sniffing around my sister, don't you?"

I did. Sandra was a beautiful high school teenage girl. She was a cheerleader when a man ten years her senior whistled at her on her way home from school one day. She was like a beautiful butterfly stuck in a black widow spider's web. Within a year, Pimpin' Easy had her out on the track, prostituting herself or "hoing" as Drama put it.

"My sister. My sister," he said. Tears filled Drama's eyes. He sat back on one elbow. He avoided my gaze, staring at the streets in front of him. "I should have killed that sucker as soon as he gave her a second glance."

I nudged his arm with my elbow. "Man, we were just kids. What could we have done?"

"I should have waited till that nigga dozed off one day and crept up and cut his damn throat with a straight razor…. Yeah, Firstborn, I do have my regrets."

We sat in silence. A black '68 Camaro rolled by. Snoop Dogg's song, "Murder Was the Case," boomed out of the truck. Drama nodded to the beat until the car sped out of sound range. "It's a sign," he said. "Snoop's talking to me."

"Snoop Dogg is in Long Beach. That's an 8-hour drive, Drama. Neither you or I have ever been that far from Oakland. How can Snoop be talking to you, man?" I asked.

Drama wiped his eyes with the back of his hand. He sniffled. "I got a letter from Lefty, man," he said.

Lefty was a triple OG from our hood serving life in prison.

"What was Lefty talking about, D?"

"He was talking about the Bible, man – Lazarus and the rich man. There was a beggar named Lazarus who used to sit at a rich man's gate begging for crumbs every day. That rich man wasn't breakin' off nothin'. He said, 'I got mine, nigga, get yours.' One day they both died. The beggar ended up in heaven. The rich man went to hell. And when he was down in the flames, he looked at Abraham up in paradise. He said, 'Abraham, send Lazarus back to earth to tell my brothers not to come to this place of torment.'

"Lefty was pretty much warning me that I was headed to the hell on earth where he was at and to turn off the highway before I got caught up forever."

"What do you think?" I asked.

"Think about what?"

"What do you think about what Lefty wrote you?"

Drama shrugged. "There ain' no exit on this road. I don't think I could get off it if I wanted to."

"Sure you could, if you wanted to."

Drama wiped the last tear from his eyes.

"If something happens to me, look in on my mama and Sandra from time to time."

"I already told you I would," I said. "What about Crayon, man?"

Drama reached in his pocket for a plastic bag filled with 'dro. He rolled himself a fat blunt.

"I can't just send the homies on that mission. Shoot, if I put a green light on everybody I had hate for, Oakland would look like the Mojave Desert. For this one, the homies have to have a say one way or the other. We going to get with the fellas later and discuss it.

Drama started singing Snoop Dogg's song, "Murder Was the Case." I joined in and sang along. I knew all of the words.

CHAPTER
NINETEEN

THE PHONE CALL CAME ABOUT MIDNIGHT. I WAS IN BED STARING at the ceiling. Mamacide, who was not known for her long conversations, said simply, "Be downstairs in five minutes. Don't make me wait." I shivered when the phone went dead. She said five. I was in front of the building in four.

The silver Infinity coupe pulled up in front of the building at exactly 12:05 p.m. The night was alive with hip hop, fire-engine sirens, and speeding cars. I opened the passenger door and hopped inside. Mamacide cut her eyes in my direction and sneered before she pulled off.

"What's up?" I asked as I buckled my seat belt.

She gave a mean chuckle. "Real niggas is up. I don't know where that leaves you though."

I sighed. I couldn't stand her.

We pulled up to the foreclosed house on Avenue D that the Black Christmas Mob illegally occupied. Mamacide hardly slowed the car. It was still drifting when she pulled close to the curb and pointed.

"Can you stop so I can get out? Damn!" I said.

She turned up E-40's jam, "Over the Stove," to let everybody know that we had arrived. As soon as I shut the door, she raced off into the night. I was left alone in the street.

There were no cars in front of the house. As I drew close to the back entrance, I could see a single candle flame in a kitchen window. Before I could knock, the door flew open. A hand grabbed my arm and yanked me into the interior darkness. The door closed behind me.

There was hardware everywhere: Tech .9s, .9mm pistols, an Uzi, and an AR-15.

Petey petted the barrel of a black straight-out-of-the-box AK-47 like it was a pregnant rattlesnake's belly. Somebody had scratched the words "BAD NEWS" on the trigger.

"What up, my nigga?" Petey asked.

"Real niggas is up," I said.

Drama's cousin, Ready, was seated at Drama's left hand. He was a crack dealer from off the streets of Richmond, California. He had deep-set green eyes that smoldered like fire embers in the candlelight. They say he slept with those eyes open. Drama used Ready when he needed somebody who could walk around the hood unrecognized. When Ready showed up in Oakland, it usually meant that somebody was about to get murdered.

"What's happening, Ready?" I asked.

Ready rose from his seat and threw his arms around my neck.

"What's crackin', big daddy?" he asked. "I ain't see you in a long time. I hear you been at college, and I don't get over this side a whole lot."

Grimy Greg said, "Ready, I'm surprised to see you in the Town."

Ready laughed, "Shoot, man it won't hurt me to get outta Richmond for a while."

Drama playfully rolled his eyes in Ready's direction, then said, "Yeah, it might not hurt you, but it'll be tough on the crack heads."

The room rocked with laughter. Drama loved his cousin and was forever teasing him. For his part, Ready was pretty good-natured about Drama's constant ribbing. Drama was probably the only person on Earth who could get away with some of the things he said to Ready. As they say, "You can pick your friends, but you can't pick your relatives."

That night Drama was animated. Adrenaline had him jumping from one subject to another. "Y'all see this shirt?" he asked. It was a shiny, black button-down shirt; something you might wear to a nightclub.

"I got it from Macy's," Drama said. "Guess, how much I paid for it."

Ready ventured a conservative guess.

"Nigga, you crazy! That's what you paid for that hoodie you got on!" Drama said.

The shirt cost an obscene amount of money. War Thug whistled when Drama pulled the price tag out of his wallet.

Ready changed the subject. "Drama, get in here and quarterback this thing, man. I can't be here all night. My wife is looking for me to be home at a decent hour," Ready said.

Drama's eyes fluttered. It was as though he couldn't believe his ears. He spoke without looking directly at Ready. "Your wife? Now Ready, I been knowing you all my life. We was in the same crib together as babies. Our mothers is sisters and they talk several times every day. And I ain't never heard no talk about no wedding. Where you get a wife from?"

Ready took a deep, patient breath. "We ain't like city hall married, but she my…"

Drama gave a deep belly laugh. "You not talking about that chick I saw you with at Denny's is you? I looked at her and thought to myself, damn, no wonder my cousin ain' never got no money. That babe looked like she sure could put it away."

I didn't want to laugh, but I couldn't help it.

"Be that as it may, Drama, I got to get home. She looking for me to be home in a couple of hours," Ready said.

Drama sat back and clutched his chest like he was having a heart attack. "I know that wasn't my flesh and blood cousin announcing that one of these broke-down broads done slapped a curfew on his butt," he said.

Ready got this exasperated look on his face, and once again I almost fell off my chair laughing.

"Well, first cousin, we ain't all got it like you," Ready said to Drama.

"You got that right!" Drama said. "That'll be the day, when one of these boppers gives me a get-home time. Y'all be taking these gold diggers out to eat, spending money. That's hella weak. I ain't bought a pair of sneakers since eighth grade…. You gotta get home," Drama mocked. "Ready, that's a damn shame!"

"Well, be that as it may, Dramacidal. Stop playing and make the shot call because I got to get back," Ready said.

Drama wiped tears of laughter from his eyes. It was time for him to get serious. "All right, listen up, y'all," he said leaning forward. "My man, Firstborn, want us to knock a nigga down."

Petey stood up and started toward the door. "Let's go," he said. "You know I'm all about that action," he said.

Drama motioned for Petey to sit back down.

"This is a little more complicated than that Petey. You see, Firstborn want us to go at Phenomenal."

Petey cocked his head to one side. "What, that supposed to mean something to me?"

"Don't you even want to know why you fixin' to scrape this nigga?" Drama asked.

Petey shrugged, "I'm not really even giving a…"

Grimy Greg interrupted. "Tell us why, D."

"This nigga Phenomenal got Maggie's niece, Crayon, out on the block hoing for him."

Grimy Greg's eyebrows knit themselves into a knot. Drama was crossing up two rules he had grown up with: mind your own business and live and let live.

"She a ho, man," Grimy said. "If that's how she get down, that's how she get down. And if that's how Phenomenal git his money, that's how he get it. I ain't one to look in the next man's pockets, unless I'm robbing him. Who am I to judge that nigga, D?"

Next it was Ready's turn. "Drama, y'all want to get at this fool 'cause he pimpin'? Nigga, you a pimp! You just told me you ain't bought a pair of sneakers since the eighth grade. Who buying those Jordans for you?"

"That ain't pimpin'," Drama said.

"Sure it is, first cousin," Ready responded. "A bitch want your time, she gotta pay for it. That's how a pimp operates. How many times you told me, 'A hustler don't fall in love.' Drama, I'm with you till the wheels fall off, but you ain't no better than Phenomenal. You ain't got no respect for women at all."

This wasn't going well. My heart started beating faster. What would happen if I couldn't get a consensus here? How would I be able to get Crayon away from Phenomenal?

Drama looked at War Thug. "What you think, homie?"

War Thug's top lip curled. "That nigga Phenomenal let our fallen homie's name come out of his mouth wrong. He got to be dealt with. I'm riding for Chopper, no matter what y'all decide."

Ready crooked his head around Drama so that he could look directly at me. "What Malcolm X over there got to say?"

Ready called me Malcolm X because my father had been a black revolutionary. Some of my relatives had been deeply involved in the Black Panther Party for Self Defense. Ready had read a lot about black history when he was locked up in the pen. When he first came home, he'd ask me lots of questions. The room got extra quiet as I started formulating my argument.

"Well since the name Malcolm X has been evoked," I said, "I'm going to quote the shining black prince. He said, 'No nation can rise higher than its women.' If we treat our women like hos, chickenheads, and bitches, we're damning ourselves. Brothers, one out of every three black men is under the supervision of the criminal justice system. We are leaving our babies to be raised by the state and attacked by the wolves. The black race is going to be extinct one day if we don't do something. And this is where we can do it. Crayon is a child. No matter what you think she looks like, she's got a child's mind and a child's heart. I need you to do this for our people. Do it for the children. Do it for me."

It was super silent for a moment. The only sound you could hear was Drama dragging on his cigarette. "How you want to do this, homie?" he asked.

"I need to be able to get close enough to talk to Phenomenal. We need to persuade him to tell us where the girl is."

"Talk!" Drama exclaimed. "No. We gotta feed that nigga what he eat." He was fixing a black bandana over the bottom of his face. "Time for talking is over. I'ma just keep it real with you. I let you give your little speech and all, but the truth is when I found out that the nigga had put his hands on you...when I found out what he said about Chopper...I had made my decision right then and there."

"That's what I'm saying," Grimy Greg chimed in.

"No!" I said trying to interject a little more bass into my voice. "We need to find out where he has the girl. We need to give him a chance to act right before we make it real for him."

"What if he don't want to act right?" War thug asked.

"Then we body his ass," Drama said. I could hear a drop of exasperation in his voice.

Drama got up from his chair and made his way to the door. We followed him. Conversation time was over. I blew out the candle and made my way out into the darkness.

The guns were tucked way. Petey toted the AK-47 under a pile of pink baby blankets. When we reached the street, he and Grimy Greg walked over to a black van with shaded windows. Virus took the shotgun seat. The rest of us piled in. War Thug turned the engine over, and we pulled away from the curb. Drama had made the shot call. It was on.

"MY BEST CHANCE OF COMING BACK ALIVE WAS TO HAVE DRAMA BY MY SIDE. IF SOMETHING WENT WRONG, HE'D KNOW WHAT TO DO."

CHAPTER
TWENTY

THE INTELLIGENCE REPORT WAS RIGHT. OUR VAN FOLLOWED A heavy string of traffic past a crowded street corner. A gang of young black men were standing in the dark beneath a burned out streetlight. The young brother with the long blond dreads was absolutely clueless that his soul might be required of him in hell that night. He couldn't see inside the van. He didn't know who was in there. He took a sip from a bottle of Olde English and passed it to one of his friends. We drove up the block and around the corner. Drama interrupted my thoughts. "So you want to talk, huh?

"That's how we have to do this, Drama," I said.

He shook his head, "Firstborn, you're crossing up all the rules of the game, but it's your call."

Petey snarled, "I don't like it. Drama, you walk up on him in the middle of the night with a rag on your face, he and his soldiers are gonna started blasting. But you take that rag off, and he still might start shooting 'cause everybody in the Town knows who you are and what you look like. I think we should make once around the block, spray them niggas up, and let it be what it is."

Drama turned around in his seat and asked, "Firstborn, how it goin' down?"

I knew we were taking a chance. Phenomenal was a gangster for real. For a minute, I thought about telling War Thug to come with me and telling Drama to stay in the car. I changed my mind. My best chance of coming back alive was to have Drama by my side. If something went wrong, he'd know what to do.

"Me and you man. That's how I want to do it," I said.

Drama decided not to carry a gun. If we lived long enough to get close to them, they'd search us. He didn't want to give them a reason to kill us. Of course, in the streets just the fact that we were where we didn't belong would have been reason enough. We were taking chances. The van came to a stop up the block and around the corner from where we'd seen Phenomenal and his boys.

Drama nodded slowly twice and then opened the van door. We all piled out. Ready knelt down next to Drama. He rolled up Drama's pant leg. From his own pocket he yanked a hunting knife with an 8" blade. He produced a roll of duct tape and taped the knife to Drama's shin. When he was finished, he pulled the pant leg down and straightened the material so the blade couldn't readily be seen. "First cousin, put this between that fool's ribs," Ready said.

Drama nodded in Phenomenal's direction and took a deep, deep breath. "Let's do it," he said.

They were standing under a broken streetlight about half a block away. The shadows froze as soon as they saw us turn the corner and walk up the block toward them. I had never been shot. I held myself tight, waiting for the deafening roar of gunfire. We drew closer and closer. Finally, I was close enough to make out Phenomenal's face in the darkness. I saw him stretch for something inside a nearby bush. Two of his dudes started reaching for their waistbands.

"Chill. We just come to talk," Drama said loud enough for them to hear. He turned to me and whispered, "Put your hands in the air, Firstborn. These boys look paranoid."

They raced over us to. A tall kid with a bullet hole scar in his cheek started patting us down.

A .38 dangled from Phenomenal's right hand. He instantly started talking garbage. "I can't believe this. Drama, come to see me? You washed up Black Christmas Mob niggas came over here and don't have a gun between the two of you. What you wanna talk about?"

"Where's the girl?" Drama asked.

"What business of yours is that, lame?"

"She's family. We don't want any trouble. Just tell us where the girl's at?"

Phenomenal's eyes turned red with rage. He cursed Drama with language I had never heard anyone ever use when they were talking to him face to face. And then a goon standing behind us grabbed Drama's arms. I let off a left hook that slammed against the side of the kid's head. He cursed me but he wouldn't let go. Before I could throw another one, two of them pulled me away from Drama's side. Phenomenal slapped Drama across the face hard as the big homie struggled to free himself. Drama shook his head like he was trying to spit out poison. I wanted to yell for help, but one of them had slapped his sour tasting hand over my mouth. He was pulling my throat backward.

Phenomenal grabbed Drama's collar. His brand new black shirt collar ripped almost clean off. I saw Phenomenal's .38 raise up in the air. I bit the hand over my mouth until the blood ran. The kid screamed in pain. I took a deep breath and hollered out into the night, "Help! Help!" I shouted.

"They got Drama!" someone down the block screamed. And then I heard the 55-round magazine cartridge slap in the AK's belly.

CHAPTER
TWENTY-ONE

WHEN THE MOB SAW THAT DRAMA WAS IN TROUBLE, THE GUNS came out, no questions asked. I could see them running toward us. Bullets started banging out. Store windows exploded. Car alarms sounded. The block was alive with gunshots. Phenomenal and his team were caught completely off guard. He dropped his gun. His team fled.

Phenomenal released Drama and tried to make a run for it. It was too late. Our niggas were on him by that time. They were pushing each other out of the way fighting for the chance to punch him in the head. When he slipped down they started stomping him. At one point, he managed to scramble to his feet and run a few steps. "Get on that nigga's head. He tryin' to run!" Drama hollered.

A woman's voice screamed from across the street, "Where's Black Hole? They whopping Phenomenal's ass."

"That nigga ripped my brand new shirt!" Drama said. "Let me get in here!"

I pulled Drama's arm before he could get into the melee. "Dude, the pigs will be on us in a minute. We got to get up out of here," I said.

Drama pointed at Phenomenal. "Take him with us. I'll bet when I get through with him, he'll be glad to tell me where the girl is."

Phenomenal's eyes were black and bulging out of his head. His lips were bruised and swollen. He put his palms up in the air. "No, no!" he said. "I don't want to go nowhere."

"Don't tell me no, bitch," Drama said.

Phenomenal seemed disoriented. "I don't want to go nowhere."

Drama sucked his teeth. "I ain't got time for this. Somebody give me a gun."

War Thug handed Drama his pistol.

"You picked the wrong set of 'washed up niggas' to play with," Drama said. And then he slammed Phenomenal over the head with the pistol butt. Phenomenal moaned. He was barely conscious. Grimy Greg and Virus poured his limp body into the van. As we sped off into the night, Drama had only one thing to say. "I can't believe that nigga ripped my brand new shirt!"

Phenomenal sat in the back seat sandwiched between Petey and Virus. Duct tape encircled his wrists. Phenomenal's lips were swollen. Both eyes were black. Blood still flowed from his head wound. He was trembling.

"Don't kill me," he begged.

"Shut the hell up, bitch!" Drama said.

"No, don't kill me," Phenomenal whined.

Ready, who sat directly behind Phenomenal laughed.

"You deserve killing," Drama told Phenomenal in a matter-of-fact manner.

In 10 minutes, we were back in East Oakland. War Thug made a right on Ritchie Street.

Ready grabbed a handful of Phenomenal's dreadlocks and almost pulled him over the seat. He pressed a .9mm pistol up against his neck. "You know that's my flesh and blood cousin you was jumping on back there. I ain't like him or Firstborn. Where I come from, we do more shooting than talking. So I'm going to ask you one question. If you give me the right answer you get to leave here tonight with your life. If you lie to me or say something other than what I want to hear, I will shoot you in your head, toss you out of this van, and then go buy myself some barbecue to take home to my woman. Listen close, 'cause I'm only asking once. Where is the girl?"

War Thug was circling for a place to toss the body should we need to kill him. We were on Seminary Avenue now.

"I've got money," Phenomenal said.

Ready's eyebrows raised; I sensed some impatience. He pressed his head forward and whispered into Phenomenal's ear. "Fool, I want to know where the girl is. I'm ready to pop a hot one off in your dome," he hissed.

Drama's ears lifted up half an inch. "Wait. Now hold up a minute, first cousin," he said. "Let me hear what playa got to say."

Sensing a chance to stay alive, Phenomenal talked fast. "I'll pay. My peoples will pay to get me back."

Drama looked at his watch. "I wonder who won the game tonight?" he asked. "Petey, you know? The A's ain't been doin' so good lately."

"I'm telling you they'll pay to get me back," Phenomenal pleaded.

"Kidnapping. I don't know. I don't like it. On the TV, it looks like the people always get caught. It's too messy," Drama said.

Of course, Drama really didn't mean any of that. When Phenomenal mentioned the magic word, "money," Drama's mind was going into fourth gear. He was thinking how he could milk this thing for a dollar. I'm telling you, when you grow up around somebody, you know how they think.

"Hey, I got an idea," Drama said.

Ready released Phenomenal's dreads. Phenomenal stared at Drama like he was a warden deliberating on whether to flip the switch on the electric chair.

"I'm going to tell my man here to let you out of the car in a few minutes," Drama said. "And I'm going to let you go back to your life just like you had it before. No problem. You can tell your niggas anything. Tell them you beat the hell out of Drama and then escaped. I don't give a damn…. The thing is, we gonna tax you."

Phenomenal's eyebrows knit together. He was a greedy man. Even with his life hanging in the balance, he wanted to ask questions about money. "How much?"

Drama said a number with a dollar sign in front. Phenomenal's eyes spread wide. "That much?" he said.

"How much is your life worth?" Drama reasoned. "Oh, yeah, and you out of the little girl business from now on."

Phenomenal nodded.

"Last thing: Tell us where Crayon is."

We made a right on East 98th.

"My brother got her. She's at the airport in Frisco. He taking her on the red-eye to Vegas. They going on United. The flight's taking off in about an hour," Phenomenal answered.

There was a brief silence in the van. Grimy Greg shuddered. "This nigga just gave up his own brother."

Phenomenal's head dropped. His chin fell onto his chest.

Drama reached over and flipped on classic soul radio. Stacy Lattishaw was signing, "I Found Love on a Two-Way Street." "Well, let's check it out," Drama said. "War Thug, we headed for the airport."

War Thug turned toward 580. We passed the back of the Coliseum. Soon we had left Oakland and had hit the gigantic span bridge that leads to San Francisco. We could see the San Francisco skyline lights in the distance. The traffic buzzed all around us.

Drama turned around to face Phenomenal. "Well bruh, I guess our business here is finished. My nigga, Petey will come see you in a few days when you get out of the hospital, and he'll get our first payment."

"Out the hospital? Why I'ma be in the hospital?" Phenomenal asked.

Drama pulled up his pant leg and ripped the knife free of the duct tape. He raised it up in the air. Phenomenal screamed as the sharp blade plunged right through his thigh. Drama pushed it down to the hilt and then pulled it out again. He wiped the blood off on Phenomenal's shirt, and then he handed the blade back to his cousin, Ready.

I was as shocked as Phenomenal. I covered my ears to block out the screaming. A Corvette Stingray passed us doing a hundred, easy.

"Now, get out pimpin'," Drama said.

"Slow down. Slow down. I'll get out," Phenomenal begged as he rocked back and forth, unable to reach the wound with his hands duct-taped behind him.

Virus opened the van door. He stood up so there was nothing between Phenomenal and cold San Francisco air. A sea of cars sped by with a deafening roar.

"And another thing. If you ever even look at my nigga Firstborn wrong, I'll kill up your whole Zip Code. Now get out, fool!" Drama shouted.

War Thug slowed. He was in a merciful mood. Maybe it was the money that had just been promised. He slowed, but he never stopped. We were doing about 25 miles an hour when

Virus and Petey kicked Phenomenal out of the van with his hands tied behind his back.

I watched Phenomenal as he rolled about eight times and then hit a wall. He squirmed in his bonds and made it to his knees and then his feet. Speeding cars swerved to avoid him. "It's hard to kill a cockroach," War Thug said.

Drama rolled the window down. He stuck his head out and hollered, "And I want a new shirt, bitch!"

Everyone laughed.

CHAPTER
TWENTY-TWO

PHENOMENAL'S ABRUPT DEPARTURE ALLOWED US TO SET OUR undivided attention on rescuing Crayon. Black Hole would be harder to deal with than Phenomenal, but there were seven of us, and by now I don't have to tell you who I was rocking with.

Still, I bowed my head and did something I've done only a few times in my life. Mostly, I just mimicked what I had seen Oliver do. I prayed silently. "Dear God, let me be able to snatch this girl out of this terrible situation. In Jesus's name. Amen."

When I opened my eyes, Drama was staring at me. All of the hardness had fled from his eyes. "Praying?" he asked.

I nodded.

"War Thug, pull over to the side of the road here," Drama ordered.

Why were we stopping? Time was of the essence. But Petey obeyed without question. The car zoomed over to the shoulder of the road. The lights went off. Before I could open my mouth to question, I saw the glow of headlights flooding the inside of our car. There was a car behind us. The police, I thought. My heart sank. There was blood and there were guns in the car. I was going to jail for the first time. Someone grabbed my door handle. I tried to remember everything that Drama had said: "Don't say anything to anybody but the lawyer. Don't listen to any promises. Ignore all the threats...."

The door opened.

It wasn't the police. Far from it. It was Oliver.

"They been following us since we left the Deep East," Drama said.

It was then I realized something both Oliver and Drama had been telling me for a long time. I wasn't right for the streets. I just didn't have the heightened instinct that you need to survive in that world. We had been followed for miles after the commission of what some might describe as a felony, and yet I had not seen the vehicle behind us.

Drama, on the other hand, had seen all of this coming and was preparing to make it work.

Oliver looked at each of us and shook his head.

"Evening, OG," Drama said with a cocky grin.

"Get out, Firstborn," Oliver ordered.

I started to argue, but Drama cut me off. "Go with OG here, Firstborn. This dude is on your team for real. If I had a mentor like him, ain't no telling where I might be. This cat really wants to see you make it. So do I. And the thing is, we can't get anywhere near that airport. You got known felons on parole in this car. Plus, they got cameras everywhere up in the place. And we can't take these guns through the metal detectors. I've taken you as far as I can. I do believe that OG here, can get it done."

Drama looked at Oliver and asked, "Ain't that right, OG?"

Oliver's eyes softened. "The boy knows I'm here for him."

I embraced Drama. My eyes filled with tears. I slapped Petey and War Thug on their shoulders. I shook hands with

Ready, Virus, Petey, and Grimy Greg. My comrades had put their lives and freedom on the line for me that night. I wanted to say thank you. I wanted to say goodbye. But I was so full of emotion I was afraid I might start crying. They all nodded. They understood.

I felt the chill in the night air as I opened the door and put my foot down on the pavement. I followed Oliver back to the Range Rover without a word. Instantly, I recognized the figure in the front seat. It was Reverend Ray, the pastor. I opened the back door and hopped in.

"Hello, Brother Firstborn," he said. Oliver cut off any further conversation. "So what's the deal?" he asked.

"They're at San Francisco Airport. Black Hole is taking her to Vegas on the red eye flight – United. We only have 19 minutes to get there if we ever want to see Crayon again. I wonder if we can make it."

Oliver started the vehicle and stomped out onto the highway. My heartbeat sped up 10 beats per minute as we swerved in and out of traffic. We entered the city limits doing 95 miles an hour. Still, I wondered if there would be enough time.

Seemingly unconcerned by our high speed, the Reverend was humming "Amazing Grace." He broke the suspense-filled atmosphere with these words: "You know, I've been sitting here thinking about my sermon for next Sunday. Y'all wanna hear what it's about?"

"You mean right now, Reverend?" Oliver asked.

"Sure." Reverend Ray didn't wait for approval. He folded his hands behind his head. Staring forward he said: "The ancient Romans were masters at turning civilized people into slaves. The whole state of Rome survived on taxes. The Romans didn't show up with an army and say, 'Pay us or die!' They hired people from among the conquered nations to raise the taxes. They'd tell some tax man, charge whatever you want. Just give us such and such amount every month.

"That system created a lot of crooks. And these Uncle Toms would get rich extorting their own people. In the Bible, we find the story of Zacchaeus the tax collector. That boy was crooked as a snake. He was all about that cheddar.

"One day, he heard that Jesus was coming to his town. As the big parade drew close, the people moved in front of him. He was a short brother. So in order to see, he had to climb a tree. When Jesus got close, he looked up and said, 'Zach baby, come on down. We having fried chicken and collar greens at your house today!'

"Zaccheus was an enemy of the state. He collaborated with the Romans to hold his own people down. He was hated. And yet, Jesus walked past all of 'the good people' to invite himself to Zaccheus's house for dinner. Zach was so moved that he said, 'Jesus, if I've robbed anybody, I'll give them a 50% return on what I stole.' The law of Moses required only 10%. Zach was saying, 'I'm all in. I want to be righteous.'

"At the end of the story, Jesus said, 'The son of man is come to seek and to save that which was lost.' Jesus was the way back for this lost brother. He's the way back for all of the lost brothers...brothers like Drama and Phenomenal. He was the way back for a brother like me. Man, it's good to be saved."

By the time the Reverend had arrived at that point in the story, we were pulling up to the San Francisco airport entrance. Oliver drove into an open parking space. He pulled his dreadlocks back and flipped a rubber band around them. He didn't want anything to get in his way if he had to get busy.

The three of us trotted through the terminal doors. We were searching for a very large man with a pretty little girl in tow. We passed concession stands, bars, and magazine shops. The pastor's shout caused my heart to leap into my throat.

"There they are!" he hollered. I saw Black Hole sitting in the waiting area. His head was bowed. His right arm was in a black sling. Thick bandages covered his arm where I had chopped him with that butcher knife. Crayon sat next to him. She looked miserable.

Oliver took off toward them. I could hardly catch him.

The giant must have heard our footsteps. He jumped to his feet.

Crayon's eyes met mine, and she smiled. "I prayed you'd come, Uncle Firstborn," she said.

"What y'all want?" Black Hole growled.

Oliver immediately started taking off his jacket. He never took his eyes off Black Hole. "I ain't here for games," Oliver said. "We want the girl. Now, we can handle this like gentlemen, or I can gorilla stomp you in front of all these people."

Black Hole jumped to his feet. "All I got to do is make the call. My soldiers will be straight up here. You don't want that OG," he said. He grabbed Crayon by the arm. His fingers fit completely around her bicep.

"Let 'em come," Oliver said. "You'll have your head twisted off your shoulders before they can get here, all the way from Oakland."

About a dozen or so white passengers stirred at the sound of two black men raising their voices. A white-haired woman with pearls around her neck grabbed her suitcase and raced away, her elderly husband in tow. A woman and five children followed a thin man in a "Boise is for Lovers" T-shirt. They're going to get the police, I thought.

Oliver balled up his fists and started toward Black Hole. The preacher ran into the bar and grill. He was back in a flash – running, with a metal bar stool hoisted over his head.

"Hold it right there!" he hollered. "Let that girl go or I'll bash in your skull and pray for forgiveness later. Let her go!"

Black Hole's massive head sank. He was like a man coming out of a deep sleep. Reality set in. He wasn't going to be able to fight all three of us with one good arm. That meant he wasn't going to get on that flight with Crayon. It was over. Crayon yanked free and ran to my side.

Black Hole looked at the preacher and just shook his head. "I know who you are, preacher. When I was young, I'd be grinding all night on the corner, but at 11:00 on Sunday morning I'd go to hear you preach."

"You'd go to church as foul as you living, homie?" I asked.

Black Hole looked at me and said, "Everybody want to hear what God has to say."

And then he simply walked away. I was glad. I was bracing for a heart attack.

"Reverend Ray, you can put the chair down," Oliver said. Reverend Ray said, "Huh?" He was like a man in a trance. He put the chair down and started laughing. We all laughed. Crayon was safe and the hell storm had passed. I looked up toward the ceiling and said, "Rest in peace, Maggie. We did it.

CHAPTER
EPILOGUE

At Debra Thursday's urging, Liza took Crayon to a safe house somewhere far away from Oakland. I stayed at Ms. Holmes' apartment for two more days. It was amazing how her mood changed. She was a woman brought back from the dead. The night before I planned to leave, the phone rang. It was Mamacide. "What's poppin', First? she asked. "Meet me downstairs in 5 minutes."

Just when I thought I was out....

Mamacide was wordless as we swerved through the streets. We stopped at the foreclosed house that Drama was using as his headquarters.

Virus was standing in front of the shuttered frame house when we drove up. He turned his back, expecting me to follow him toward the rear of the building. He went through the back door, and I followed.

The first thing I noticed were the two long braids that hung down over Drama's Oakland Raiders game jersey. He stepped out of the shadows bobbing his head to NWA's, "100 Miles and Running." I'm sure he was aware of my presence in the airless box, but he never so much as nodded in my direction.

The room was as dark as a burned-out planet. I could hear the scamper of feet darting purposefully behind a bed sheet that separated the kitchen from the living room. Petey's silhouette stood at the door cradling the AK-47 assault rifle like a newborn baby with a banana clip in its mouth. A shadow detached itself from the wall and sauntered into the room.

There was someone in the living room. Drama pulled the bed sheet back and beckoned me to follow him into the living room.

I gasped. There was a law enforcement officer sitting on the couch. The man in the uniform sucked all of the deadly nutrients out of a glass pipe. Grimy Greg popped another rock in. The officer looked up to Drama with pleading eyes after the last hit had drained dry from the glass gas chamber.

"One of y'all hit my man here with three or four more of them things. And where's the Remy Martin? Don't even front, yo. Tighten my man up, here dude," Drama said.

This was not good at all. My first thought was to hit the door and run for my life. Petey must have anticipated my thoughts. He blocked the exit.

In the darkness, a hand holding an open bottle of spring water stretched out. The cop snatched the container. He twisted the top off, gulped, then shook his head.

"Drama, what's in this bottle? My head is spinning," he said.

A few chuckles sprinkled throughout the room.

"Thizz is what it is my man. That's thizz water. It's crushed up E pills in there," Drama said. Small, undissolved lavendar-colored chunks swam around in the bottom of the bottle.

"Wha...?"

"Ecstasy pills."

"I don't mess with no ecstasy. Only cocaine," the cop said.

"Drink up, dawg. It's our treat," Drama said, generosity twinkling in his eyes.

The officer gulped down the whole bottle and then collapsed back on the filthy couch. He told us his bank account number. He told us his ATM pin code, where his mother lived, where his woman lived, and where his kids went to preschool. All of this with his eyes closed.

Drama laughed like a madman.

"Do you know what the hell you're doing, man?" I asked. "You're shooting dice with the devil on the ledge of the bottomless pit!"

Drama ignored me. "So, officer, tell me what's up with Street Life."

"Who?" the officer said. He wiped his lips with the back of his hand.

Drama's patience had worn thin very quickly. "Street Life ...fool. Wake yourself up, clown. You know our nigga that's doin' time where you at. What's up with Life?"

"I'm under oath not to talk about things that happen at my job," the officer said.

Drama clucked his tongue against the roof of his mouth and rolled his eyes. He looked back at his soldiers.

"Somebody hit my man off with one of those fat ones... the ones we save for our good customers."

Virus dropped three pieces of crack into the officer's hand. The cop stuffed one of them into the stem and blew up the end with a torch.

"It's good, Drama," the officer said.

Drama bounced down on the couch next to the officer. He twirled his hands around in a tumbling motion, inviting the officer to talk. "You was saying about my homeboy, Street Life."

"Oh, yeah, they had your boy in the administrative segregation unit. He couldn't go nowhere without two deputies.

But now they got him moved in with the general population. I had to write him up because he slapped another inmate in the head with a phone and said, 'This phone belongs to the brothers.'

"He can't see me 'cause I'm looking down at him through the one-way glass, but I can see him, jogging in place, politicking with the young thugs. He's a legend in there ya know. It's the strangest thing. He's got the word "HELLBOUND" tattooed on his stomach. I tell you, Drama, he's gonna come back and start war down here. I wouldn't be surprised if he killed you."

Street Life was the third founding member of Black Christmas Mob. He was the muscle. He was truly about what he said he was about. That was how he got that name.

In fact, Street Life's name came up in many an unsolved murder investigation. Drama was deeply concerned about the suggestion that Street Life was about to see daylight again.

"Street Life ain't coming back from the dead. I was there when they gave the nigga 25 to life," Drama declared.

"Overturned on a technicality," the officer said. "Yeah, he's sitting up on those little round stainless-steel stools playing cards on the stainless-steel countertop in his blue, one-size-fits-all two-piece. Yeah, he's just sitting there waiting for a release date. It should be any day now."

"Who's with him?" Drama asked.

"All your enemies," the guard said. He took a big gulp from the spring water bottle.

"They say they gon' kill you, Drama. Street Life says you set him up. He comin' out and he gon' blast you to kingdom come. He gon' leave your brains hanging out."

War Thug's eyes narrowed.

"Have another swig of that thizz water," Drama said.

"I can't think straight, now," he said.

"That's all right. I can do the thinking for both of us. Have another sip."

The officer obeyed. "And he gon' kill yo' partner, too. I think they're going to let him out day after tomorrow," he said.

His words began to slur.

"I imagine you're Firstborn, aren't you?" he said looking at me. The shock on my face must have told him the answer. He smiled.

Drama kicked the guard with the edge of his sneaker. "Pig, you don' come around here acksin no questions. I ask the questions. Get your punk ass up."

"I can't drive. I'm too high."

A flash like the birth of the universe splattered light in the midst of the darkness. The cop's beet-red eyes opened wide momentarily. Drama had used his cell phone to snap the officer's photograph.

"Picture time!" Drama hollered, laughing.

"What did you do, Drama? I'm finished!" the officer moaned incredulously.

The man reached his hand toward Drama and grabbed the hem of his Raiders game jersey.

"Why did you take my picture with a pipe in my hand?"

"Officer, it's just a little souvenir of our visit. Nothing to worry about, unless you refuse a favor I may come to ask you one day," Drama said.

Saliva leaked from the side of the officer's mouth. "I can't drive."

"Give your keys to Petey. He'll drive you home."

"War Thug, you follow 'em, and when he park, drive Petey back."

The officer's stuttering told me he didn't like the arrangement, but his only other option would have been to leave his car and take public transportation. In that neighborhood, at night, in that uniform? No, I don't think so.

"You did this to me on purpose, Drama. Didn't you?" the jail guard asked.

"Don't even go there. Nobody kidnapped you and brought you down here. You wanted to get high, and I accommodated you. That's what I do. I'm a pharmaceutical entrepreneur. And I don't get pleasure outta snitchin' on anybody, even cops. You just do what I tell you when I reach out to you, and that picture will never see the light of day."

The officer had to be helped to his feet.

"Oh, and Frank," Drama said in a dead pan voice, "if you tell anybody you seen me or where I'm at, that picture will be on the front cover of the newspaper the next day.

War Thug jerked his arm. "Where da keys at cop?" he demanded.

"Left pants pocket," the cop said without making a motion to retrieve them.

War Thug stuck his arm halfway in the cop's pants pocket. He pulled back keys – and a well-worn leather wallet.

"Got 'em," he said, while sticking the wallet in his own pocket. The jail guard seemed not to notice.

"See ya, Drama," he slurred.

Drama waved the back of his hand like he was trying to dispel a bad odor.

War Thug and Petey helped the cop to his feet and walked him out the back door.

Sweat trickled down my armpits. This was all bad.

"Drama, what does he mean?" I asked. "Street Life knew the risks coming in to the game. You told him not to take his girls up to the motel where we kept the stash. He ignored you, and the police set him up. Why does he want to come back to here to get at us?" I asked.

Drama shook his head. He looked tired.

"Make sure you get out of the town tomorrow, First. Street Life is going to come at us, and he's gonna come at us hard."

CAUGHT UP AND NEED HELP?

Reach out to one of the organizations below.

MISSSEY
(Motivating, Inspiring, Supporting,
and Serving Sexually Exploited Youth)
470 27th Street
Oakland, CA 94612
E-MAIL: *info@misssey.org*
CALL: (510)290-6450
WEBSITE: *www.misssey.org*

Victory Outreach of Oakland
info@vooakland.org
(510)905-6450
WEBSITE: *www.vooakland.org*

The SAGE Project
(Standing Against Global Exploitation)
1275 Mission Street
San Francisco, CA
(415)905-5050
E-MAIL: *info@sagesf.org*
WEBSITE: *www.sagesf.org*

GEMS
(Girls Educating and Mentoring Services)
WEBSITE: *www.gems-girls.org*

HOLLER AT AUTHOR, HARRY LOUIS WILLIAMS II
E-MAIL: *hoodmovement21@yahoo.com*
He'd love to hear from you.